Jungle House

Jungle House

JULIANNE PACHICO

First published in Great Britain in 2023 by Serpent's Tail,
an imprint of PROFILE BOOKS LTD
29 Cloth Fair
London
EC1A 7JQ
www.serpentstail.com

10 9 8 7 6 5 4 3 2 1

Typeset in Freight Text by MacGuru Ltd
Designed by Barneby Ltd
Printed and bound in Great Britain by Clays Ltd, Elcograf S.p.A.

A CIP record for this book can be obtained from the British Library.

ISBN: 978 1 80081 761 6
eISBN: 978 1 80081 763 0

For Nick and Pansy

Chapter One

EVERY MORNING LENA OPENS HER EYES and the day is stretched out before her and there's a lot of work that needs to be done. There's fishing and mushroom gathering and swimming in the river. Five days a week are for exercise and two days are for rest. In the orchard there are bananas and guavas, grapefruits and limes. Depending on the season, the garden will have cassava, sweet potatoes, and peppers as long and thin as her fingers. There's a reserve of rice and beans in the storeroom, but it won't last forever; it's important to follow the schedule written in her notebook. What will she do when it runs out? She rarely eats meat but a few times a month she'll take the shotgun and go hunting: deer and peccaries, tapir and agoutis. She never hunts monkeys because she can't stand the thought of their curled-up fists in the pot. There are chickens on the property, although every year they get wilder, and she more reluctant.

When she last spoke to Mother, the juvenile hawks were still fuzzy and white with their baby plumage, and the rainy season was coming to an end. That was a month ago. By now they will have fledged, their chests brown and spotted.

It's certain that Mother will be angry at her for moving into the hut – for storming off like that. But their last conversation was so hostile, it seemed best to have some space. And it wasn't like she and Mother had never fought before – my God, how they'd fought!

But they've always made up, and she doesn't see how today will be any different.

And anyway, these days Mother is angry all the time.

Since she moved out, Lena's been living in the guest hut by the orchard. 'The guest hut' isn't an accurate name because the family never hosted any guests. Decades ago, they would have hosted relatives, or colleagues, or even university researchers, but that's never happened in her lifetime. It's hard not to think of the family as guests – but then what does that make her? Perhaps 'caretaker's hut' is more accurate. Yes. And that makes her the caretaker.

The main house is much grander, but the caretaker's hut suits her fine. For one, it's out of Mother's sight. Like the main house, it's built on stilts, useful for keeping out floodwaters during the rainy season, as well as insects and snakes. While the main house is constructed out of expensive local hardwood, with the most advanced solar panels the family could get at the time, the care-taker's hut is much simpler. Palm-wood walls, palm-branch roof, all of it knotted tightly together with lianas from the jungle, as tough and scratchy as the hardened skin of her heels. She has two rooms, one for cooking and one for sleeping. There's a porch where she likes to sit in the evenings when chores are done and write in her notebook by candlelight or torch. She can write down what she's eaten that day, and what she plans to eat tomorrow. She has a kerosene lamp but rarely lights it because kerosene needs to be saved, and the number of bugs it attracts is overwhelming. She sleeps on a mattress under a mosquito net, and every morning she shakes off the spiders and lizards that fell there overnight. Occasionally there are rat droppings, but rarely.

To visit Mother, she must cross the orchard, which is by far her favourite part of the property. She's never said this to Mother, though. *Great*, Mother would say. *Wonderful. So the place that's by far the messiest and most untidy is your favourite. Isn't that lovely.* But the orchard isn't even the 'messiest' place by far – can the orchard even be considered 'messy', in comparison to the jungle?

But try telling Mother that! *Oh God,* Mother might say, *the jungle,* and then she'd be off.

But how could she explain to Mother that it's precisely because the orchard is so overgrown and disorderly that she loves it? So many rotting papayas and mangos! So many green turds from the feral pack of chickens (now generations old, a regal dynasty). Yes, she loves the orchard, every part of it, even though there are sights there that make her sad. The pit bull's grave, for one. She visits it every day. If she doesn't tend to it, the surrounding jungle devours the tiny dirt mound completely, like it wants to swallow it whole. And so she pulls away weeds and mushrooms. Shoos away beetles and centipedes. Whispers a word or two. The poor pit bull. Nobody deserved such a fate.

She won't visit him today, though. It's best to get this over with.

Her plan is to act as though everything is normal. So she heads straight to the patio chairs, more neutral ground than inside the house. As a child, she would sit here and rest after cleaning the swimming pool, and she and Mother would gossip for hours. There definitely won't be any gossip today. But she's brought the machete, in case there's a simple and straightforward task she can do for Mother, one that can be completed easily.

She takes her seat on the one chair she's successfully kept clean over the years, scrubbed free of the speckled black mould that ruthlessly attacks anything plastic. It's a Sisyphean task, but she does it dutifully. She notes with dismay the moss that's grown on the chair legs. How quickly things can change! But the pool is the same. The pool is always the same. Empty apart from the thin layer of scummy water. The hours she spent here as a child with the skimmer! The number of purple blossoms scooped from the water! The rescued baby iguanas! How Mother despised them: their tiny nails, and the stink she insisted was there, even though Mother can't smell – has never been able to.

'Mother,' she says. She doesn't raise her voice because she doesn't need to; Mother will hear. 'Mother, I'm here.'

*

A dragonfly lands on the glistening scum, before retreating immediately, as if disgusted.

'Well, Lena,' Mother says. No greeting, no *how are you*. 'So you're not dead. Apparently.'

'No.'

'No botfly eggs in your arms.'

'No.'

'No infected bites. No tapeworms.'

'Not that I know of.'

'There you go.' Mother sighs. 'At least some things are all right with the world. At least not everything is completely fucked.'

Mother rarely swears, as she considers it beneath her – she must be in a mood. And when Mother is in a mood, Lena needs to be careful. She waits patiently.

Here it comes. 'But as you can see,' Mother says, 'the nest is still there—'

Lena interrupts quickly. 'They've fledged though, haven't they?'

'Oh, Lena –' And this is it – of all things, this is what sets Mother off. There she goes, she's off now, there's no stopping her! Mother's mood, black and swirling, bearing down on Lena like an afternoon thunderstorm. 'Lena, you just can't imagine. You'll never know how awful it is. The smell, Lena. The stink!'

Again, it's a fact that Mother can't smell – but forget about bringing *that* up.

'The constant flies, Lena. Can you even see up there? The carcasses? Body parts, Lena. Feet and beaks. Feathers, Lena. And layers and layers of encrusted, hardened—'

'But Mother,' she says. She's trying to talk fast – maybe if she acts incredibly anxious, speaking a million miles a minute, this will offset Mother's own anxiety. 'Remember last year, Mother? Last year wasn't so bad, was it?'

Last year was when she went up the ladder with a pair of gardening gloves from the shed. She pulled away the worst of the nest debris, tossing it recklessly over her shoulder, secretly enjoying the mess it made as it scattered over the patio tiles. How Mother cried as the ladder wobbled! How Mother groaned at the sight of the flattened songbird carcasses, baked into stiff patties by the heat. But once Lena swept them away, Mother calmed right down.

'What *would* help,' Mother says, 'is throwing the whole nest in the river. And lining the roof with broken glass. And after that: shooting them. You're good at that, aren't you? Supposedly? Isn't that part of your so-called heritage? That's the only kind of help that would realistically do any good—'

Lena unscrews the lid of her water bottle and takes a long drink. The water is far too warm to be refreshing.

Because when Mother finishes with the hawks, next up will be the possums, who've built their own nest in the chimney. It doesn't matter that the chimney is something that the Morels have never used, and probably never will. For Mother, it's unacceptable.

'You know, Mother,' she interrupts. 'If I block it up, they'll just nest somewhere else, in a place you'll find even more unpleasant.'

But Mother isn't listening; Mother doesn't stop. What follows are the usual talking points: the warping floors, the peeling wallpaper, the stained ceiling. Corroding metal, brackish water, layers of salt crystals on the wooden beams. Mother, talking. And Lena, sitting with growing discomfort, shifting her weight from one buttock to another as Mother's litany grows and grows. The odours. My God, the odours! She knows they're there, Lena, she just knows it! 'I can feel them,' Mother frets, and this is when Lena starts to feel them too: as suffocating as steam from soup. A sour rankness she can smell, but Mother can only imagine. 'Like a gas,' Mother says. 'It stinks, Lena, it reeks. Oh, I can't bear the thought of letting you inside; it'd be far too humiliating.'

Lena should say something comforting at this point. She really should.

Instead, she uses her feet to drag the chair across the tiles, into a shadier spot provided by the grapefruit tree.

Mother has always been obsessed with keeping the house clean and the property safe. Security and order – those are Mother's jobs. Providing information as requested was another key task.

But that hasn't been the case for the past six months, since the satellite connection was lost.

Still, in the twenty years that they've known each other – the twenty years that Lena's been alive – those primary jobs haven't changed. And she, Lena – her entire life, she's always been helpful. Mother's helper.

What *has* changed – she must admit, albeit reluctantly – is the extent of Mother's rages. Especially this past year, since the Morels' last visit. Sure, Mother had always been a bit on the angry side, a bit irritable, but her temper has definitely become a bit more . . . well, pronounced. Lena's often wondered if it's a result of Mother's aloneness. Of course, *she's* been here for Mother, but it's not the same, obviously. How could Lena ever hope to replace the relationship Mother had with the satellites?

Anyway, she doesn't like to think about it, and Mother certainly would never bring it up. But when she *does* think about it, late at night in the hut, when she can't sleep – if she thinks about it too long, it becomes hard to breathe. Like her lungs have become sticky, overgrown with spiderwebs.

The satellite connection, gone. The family, silent. And Mother, alone.

It can't have been easy.

Especially with Lena moved out, on top of everything else.

And so, Mother's rages – she can't resent them. How can she? All Mother wants to do is her job – keeping the house safe, orderly and tidy. To stay busy and purposeful. Who wouldn't want that?

The Morels used to come three times a year – two weeks at Christmas, ten days at Easter and three weeks in summer. The visits decreased over the years, due to the rebels' presence in the area, which was obviously not her or Mother's fault – not anything anyone could control. During the last fateful Christmas visit – a year ago now – the family was barely here for a week, cutting their trip short. After that trip, the Morels stopped coming, and six months after that, the satellites cut off. But even when the connection was still functioning, she and Mother never heard from the Morels, not a word.

So she and Mother have had to do their best, making do with what they have. Without the satellite connection, it's impossible for Mother to receive any news, but the country must be in turmoil, what with the upcoming elections and the increasing support for the former rebel candidate. It must be the worst bump in the road since the disarmament process. And, of course, it's obvious why the family won't be returning any time soon. But who could say what the future might hold? Both Mother and Lena have lived through this kind of isolation before and come out of it just fine; now shouldn't necessarily be any different. Yes, a couple of years might pass, and when the Morels came back, things would obviously be different, but they could survive; they'd done it before. Her and Mother. The two of them could wait out anything. Any sensible person would see why the Morels need time away from the property. Lena understands, Mother understands (well . . . she *thinks* Mother understands). She doesn't hold the radio silence against the Morels; she doesn't take it personally.

Mother isn't even the family's only property. There's also Mountain House, where the family spends three-day weekends during the school year. Lena has never been to the mountains – she's never left the property – but, according to Mother, the weather there was much pleasanter. *Not a sweat fest like here, Lena – to be honest, you'd probably prefer it, it'd suit you; you'd end up never wanting to leave.* But I like it right here, Mother, she'd insist. I don't want to leave. And even if Mother didn't say anything in response, she'd know Mother was pleased. It was unfortunate that Mother's relationship with Mountain House was so acrimonious. Her most common complaint – repeated often, with much bitterness – was *He thinks he's better than me, Lena, so damn superior, and believe me, dealing with someone with that kind of personality is a complete waste of time.*

The main family home was City House, on the military base. That's where Isabella went to school – well, used to go to school – and her father to work. Mother's relationship with City House was even worse than with Mountain House. How scandalised Mother had been by what happened! *The way she admitted those rioters*, Mother once ranted. *Just let them waltz right in through the gates. She let them break the windows! She let them burn the car! Unbelievable. Unforgivable. Absolutely useless. They should have torn her apart for scrap metal. That's the only thing she's good for now.*

Mother! Lena exclaimed, alarmed by the harshness of Mother's judgement. But Mother just laughed.

But even so – even though the Morels hadn't been in touch the past year (which, while distressing, was completely understandable) – Mother had never failed to do the best job she possibly could. And Lena had too.

When Mother is off on one of her rages, all Lena can provide is an audience. And so she sits quietly, watching the hummingbirds flit back and forth across the patio. Because once Mother finishes with the smell – 'I suspect mould, or possibly mushrooms, heaven forbid!' – she'll move on to the final topic, the one that most enrages her: the jungle itself. And today is no different. If the movement of the stars above follow a regular pattern (as taught to her by Mother – *if the rebels ever snatch you, Lena, you'll find it useful*), then so do Mother's complaints.

The snakes. The bats. The bugs. In the year without the family, it's only got worse. Despite Lena's best efforts, the jungle itself is now encroaching upon Mother: vines on the drainpipe, termite nests in the ceiling. There's no escaping it; Mother can't get away.

But there are so many things in the jungle she wishes she could show Mother! Because, if Mother could see, perhaps she would change her mind. If only Mother could lie in the river and let the water carry her, thin slimy fish nibbling her underarms. If only she could shine a light under the logs and see the glistening skin of the frogs and salamanders, their cool, slow blinks, unperturbed in their damp wisdom. If only she could take Mother up the branch of that one tree she feels confident in climbing, sit there waiting patiently for the band of spider monkeys to pass by – their little wrinkled hands and the tender way they groom each other, their squashed, puckered faces.

8

But it doesn't matter, because Mother only ever notices disgusting things from the jungle. Dirty things. Like the fly larvae wiggling inside the pit bull's wound, eating him from the inside out. Oh, how Mother had shouted . . .

Mother is many things, even without the satellites, but one thing she'll always be is stuck where she is. And the satellites' absence hasn't helped, even if Mother claims that she doesn't miss them, that in fact she feels better without them – *They were getting strange, Lena, filled with abnormal ideas, and no wonder: living high up like that would make anyone go peculiar. It does things to your mind.*

'I don't know how I can take it, Lena,' Mother is saying right now. 'I don't know why I keep going.'

When this particular tone in Mother's voice arrives, it's best to interrupt. 'I can't help with the mould,' Lena says. 'I can't make it go away completely. But if you want me to remove the termite nest, I can.'

'Oh, no,' Mother says instantly. 'That would be— I'd hate to impose. You'd feel so guilty if too many died by mistake, and then you'd blame me and get pissy.'

'I won't make a mistake. I can use smoke.' She's already brainstorming techniques. Where did Alfonso leave the grill? Was it stored in the shed? A wood fire would be better, but there's no chance Mother would consent to have something like that used so close to the house . . .

'Smoke is a risk,' Mother says. 'Especially for those godforsaken hawks. If they inhale too much they'll drop dead off the roof. And then you'll get in another mood with me, and spend another month sulking in your little hut.'

Steady now, Lena tells herself. You've done great so far. Hang in there and don't crack. 'Well, if you're sure.'

'I am.'

They fall silent. The crickets and cicadas are singing in that distinct way she only ever hears here, this close to the house – the ones by the caretaker's hut (*her* hut) are shriller, more high-pitched. If she wants to stop the sun from beating down on her head, she's going to have to drag the chair towards the shade again. But instead she stands up, a bit too quickly.

'Well,' she says again, 'I'm sorry I can't stay longer—'

'Oh, no,' Mother says. 'Don't be silly.'

'Do you want me to take a look at the vines on the drainpipe? I brought the machete—' She holds it up high, like she did when she was little and wanted Mother to see a drawing she'd made, an interesting-looking rock she'd found, a piece of wood she'd carved. *Mother, look what I have!*

'The vines are fine,' Mother says. 'The drainpipe is fine. I don't know why I said anything about the vines in the first place, or the drainpipe, for that matter. There's nothing whatsoever about either the vines or the drainpipe that requires immediate attention.'

'If you're sure,' she repeats. She shifts her weight awkwardly from one foot to another. In this kind of heat she becomes painfully aware of how sweaty she must seem to Mother, how greasy. The huge pores on her nose, the stiff hairs on her chin. When she was a child, she never paid attention to these differences between her and Mother. Now, it makes her feel guilty, like she's failed to do something she was supposed to. Her body has come between them. The clumsy inelegance of such a puffy, solid form, with hands that swell up when it's too hot, menstrual cycles that last over a week, and feet that peel in the rainy season and smell like cheese.

At least Mother doesn't show her repulsion, even if she feels it. Well, apart from the occasional comment here and there.

'Actually,' Mother says, and there's a note now in Mother's voice that gives reason to pause, 'there is one thing.'

Lena stiffens. She tries not to, but it happens anyway. And Mother will notice, because Mother notices everything.

'Behind the pool,' Mother says. 'Where the old chicken coop used to be. You remember, right?'

'Of course.' Years ago, she rebuilt the coop closer to the care-taker's hut, so that the chickens were less likely to destroy the grass closest to the house.

'Something's there,' Mother says. 'In the overgrowth. The bushes, or whatever you want to call them. I have a rough guess of what it is. But I need to see to be sure.'

'What is it?'

'You'll have to go in and pull it out, so I can be certain.'

She bites the inside of her lip. This, too, Mother will notice.

'It's not like that time by the river,' Mother says. 'Okay? I promise. It's nothing like that time at all. But if you're still in a mood with me over that, Lena, then I really don't know what else I can say. My reaction back then was perfectly understandable.'

'I'm not in a mood.' The time by the river was four months ago. Mother had spotted vultures gathering by the gorge, over the private cove where Lena and Isabella used to swim, and insisted that Lena go investigate. They'd both got horribly worked up – Lena in tears, and Mother's voice angry and awful in a way Lena had never heard before. And then, after all that drama, Lena had crept down the gorge, bracing herself for a terrible sight, and terrible news to report to the family. But combing through the overgrown vegetation had revealed nothing more than the remains of a butchered goat. Mother immediately recorded it in the security logs as possible evidence of increasing rebel presence. Lena had buried the goat's remains on the riverbank, in soil that was more like clay. Digging the hole hadn't been easy, and had made no sense to Mother whatsoever (*Just throw it back in the water for the caimans! Heaven knows why the rebels dumped it; they probably pumped it full of some disgusting drug from their awful laboratories*). But Lena had dug the hole anyway, left a small dirt mound carefully marked by a pile of stones. She still visited it sometimes, after attending to the pit bull's grave.

'What really gets me,' Mother says, 'is that I have no idea how this thing got there. Whatever it is. It must have happened during one of my spells.'

Lena's breath quickens. 'Have you had one recently?'

'Oh, Lena, you know how they are; they just happen and I don't even realise it. I know how useless and incompetent you think they make me, so please don't bother telling me.'

'I wasn't planning to.'

Mother rarely mentioned her spells, but Lena feared them. They weren't as bad as Mother's moods – not as dark, not as powerful – but had far more worrying connotations. *It's like I go away and then come back, Lena. But time has passed, and I'm never sure how much, and I don't know what I've missed. But it's nothing to worry about; I'm sure it's just a way my system has adapted over the years to keep me functioning as efficiently as possible. It's a minor irritation, at best.*

Mother never seemed bothered when she discussed her spells – only matter of fact. But still. In the past year, she'd been having more and more of them. Even though Lena tried not to think about it too much, the facts were undeniable: Mother, not seeing. Mother, less effective. Mother, missing things she should have spotted right away.

Was this it, then? Had it already begun?

Mother, failing. Mother, old.

Mother no longer herself.

'It's in the bushes,' Mother says, 'and not too deep. You won't get your arms scratched. I promise. I promise.'

'Well, if you're promising twice . . .'

Mother laughs, and Lena can't help but smile.

She walks all the way around the empty pool. Mother is right, the overgrown bushes aren't that bad, especially considering how rarely they've been attended to (when was the last time Lena trimmed them back?). There are a few wooden boards scattered here and there, left over from the previous chicken coop, now exploding with orange mushrooms. These are Mother's most hated species, after the mushy brown ones. *Don't eat them, Lena, they'll give you horrible visions and make you think absurd things. Leave them for the birds, they're already insane.*

Lena stands at a distance, scanning carefully. But Mother calls out, her voice carrying across the patio, the pool, the flattened patch of grass: 'It's deep in there, Lena! You're going to have to pull some branches back!'

She does so reluctantly, trying to peer as deep into the tangled growth as she can, wincing at the occasional sharp prick of a thorn.

'There you go!' Mother says. 'Getting closer, Lena!'

With her back turned, it feels reasonably safe to roll her eyes.

'I don't see anything,' she says.

'What?'

Another potential cause for concern – is Mother's hearing fading too?

'I said, I DON'T SEE ANYTHING.' Unable to hide her impatience, she uses her boot to stomp down viciously on a branch. Stomp, stomp, stomp. This helps her move deeper into the bushes. There's something satisfying about crushing them down. Her trousers are thick and feel pleasingly protective. Like most of her clothes, they're from Isabella's closet – Isabella's jungle outfits. Thorns rasp against cloth; her forehead prickles with sweat.

'Mother, there's nothing here—'

Her foot comes into contact with something hard.

'There it is!' Mother crows. 'I knew it, I knew it!'

She has no choice other than to reach in deep. She can't help herself; she lets out a cry. Thin red lines are forming on her arms; there's definitely a spark of blood. But somehow she's able to grasp the object and pull it out.

'I knew it,' Mother is still saying. She's not shouting, but her voice is much louder than it needs to be. 'I knew it, Lena! I was right!'

The scratches on her arm are stinging. She has to rotate the item in her hands a few times before understanding what it is.

It's a pair of field binoculars. Simply designed. Black, with faint scratches across the lenses. Small enough to hold in the palm of one hand.

'Turn around.' Mother is definitely yelling now. If any birds were nearby, they'd fly away in alarm. 'Turn around and hold it up.'

Dutifully, she does. It doesn't have any straps, so she holds it with the lenses pointing up. Mother is still shouting, but for a brief second her words don't register, the words don't come through.

13

Lena has lived here all her life, and she would know if this was a pair owned by the family; she'd recognise it immediately, as she recognises all their possessions. If it were a misplaced pair from the army, dropped accidentally from one of the helicopters that still occasionally patrol overhead, it would have a military insignia, or the country's flag, some kind of logo to indicate ownership. It's also definitely not an item from the search party, because the search parties didn't use binoculars – they had their drones, and that was enough. And because it is none of those things, Lena is obliged to arrive at the same conclusion as Mother, who is still shouting words that Lena can't quite register, language Lena can't yet absorb. Because if these binoculars are from neither the family nor the military nor the search parties, then the only other reasonable explanation is that they come from a rebel, someone who was here, and close, and not that long ago.

Chapter Two

BACK WHEN THE FAMILY used to come, Lena and Mother would adjust their schedules and assume additional responsibilities. For Lena, this mainly consisted of attending to Isabella. For Mother, it consisted of directing staff, enforcing security, and looking after Isabella's parents. The Morels were predictable in the way they spent their holidays. There was wading in the river or hiking down the rocky gorge towards the private cove. There was sitting by the swimming pool and sunbathing. Best of all was birdwatching on the balcony: every night macaws flew home in pairs, and enormous flocks of swallows swarmed towards the waterfall, an hour's hike away.

Lena and Mother liked the visits. The family never demanded too much when they were there, not truly. The house itself had been in the family for generations. Isabella's mother owned the surrounding land, which long ago had been a rubber-tree plantation owned by Isabella's grandfather. Mother had never met him – she was only a few years older than Lena – but she referred to him as *Henry Senior* when she was being respectful, *Henry-the-plantation-baron* when she was being precise, and *you know, the big boss guy*, when she wasn't thinking too hard about her tone. Because of the ongoing conflict and increasing rebel presence, there was a long period when the family couldn't visit. Isabella herself hadn't come until she was seven, when Lena had just turned nine.

Of course, the family had known the whole time that Lena was there – Mother had kept them informed. Not the whole story, of course, but Mother's version of it. And once the disarmament process concluded – the year that Lena turned nine – things became safer and stabler, and the family started to come again.

Safety was the responsibility Mother took most seriously. *No peace negotiation or disarmament process in the world is ever going to change that, Lena, believe me. Bandits don't go away, criminals don't go away, shameless good-for-nothings don't go away. Potential combatants are a constant threat. I've always got to be on the lookout. I know what I'm talking about; I've seen it all. Nothing can surprise me at this point, nothing.*

The house had been designed by a famous architect, and, with the exception of its solar panels, was built entirely out of wood. It was originally constructed by Henry's Austrian great-grandfather, who'd dreamed of building a house in the middle of the forest (that was the word he'd used: 'forest', not 'jungle'). Lena knew all this from Mother's lessons, as well as the thin paper pamphlets she'd carefully flicked through, the ones that formed part of the family's extensive memorabilia about the house and its history.

There was no road access to the house. Previous inhabitants could only reach it by river, and even that fluctuated depending on the flooding season and the flowing of various tributaries. The house was two storeys high with balconies on the second floor. Connected to the house by a series of wooden walkways were several cabins, used for different purposes. There was a studio for Isabella's mother, for her watercolour painting. There was the food storeroom: beans, rice, flour, sugar, oil, powdered milk and more. There was the laundry room, which also served as storage space for non-food items. And closer to the jungle's boundary, across the orchard, was the guest hut. The caretaker's hut. Lena's hut. Behind the laundry room was the water tank, a large tower of 20,000 litres connected to a deep well. (Isabella once asked Lena if she'd ever climbed down it, and Lena had politely answered 'no'. In her head, though, she imagined Mother putting it this way: *Lena's not in the habit of doing idiotically pointless and life-risking things; it's not worth it.*) At a significant distance from the house were the landing strips for the helicopters, once maintained dutifully by Lena with intense machete-hacking sessions, but now overgrown, reclaimed by the jungle – yet another task she's let slide. *How many helicopters can fit there again, Mother? How many can come?* This was one of her favourite questions to ask as a child, a question she knew the answer to, but enjoyed seeing Mother getting worked up about. *Something like a dozen average-sized ones, Lena. Though thankfully we've never had that many come at one time – can you imagine? The noise, the mess! My nerves are barely coping as it is!*

The last time they had a helicopter land there – the family's last day. That . . . had not been a good day at all.

It delighted Lena when the family enjoyed their visits. This feeling was especially strong from the age of eleven, when Mother assigned her more responsibilities for running the household, apart from just attending to Isabella. The family's pleasure in the scenery gave Lena a sense of pride, as though she herself was personally responsible for its beauty. She loved it when they exclaimed over the hummingbirds or laughed at the squabbling howler monkeys. Mornings were for the leisure area, and afternoons were for the beach, which is what they called the patch of sand by the river. The leisure area consisted of a pier extending over the water, perfect for diving off and fishing. It also had the sauna with its panoramic view and steam room, the garage with the yacht, motorboat and jet skis, as well as the concrete ramp. There was also the canoe, tied to a fence post as it drifted in the river, but no one had touched it in years (*Lena, are you ever going to put that damn thing away? It's a wonder the wood hasn't rotted by now*).

It would take less than a day after their arrival for Isabella's skin to start burning and become swollen with blistering, angry mosquito bites. Lena's bites – on the rare occasion she got them – were never like Isabella's; at their absolute worst they were

17

small raised bumps with a red pinprick in the middle. After spotting them, Mother would always make the exact same comment: *You're lucky not to be allergic to mosquito saliva, like Isabella. You're a true child of the jungle.* And Lena would laugh awkwardly, because the way Mother said it, she could tell: it wasn't a compliment.

'Peel me, Lena!' Isabella would cry, pulling down her bathing suit straps. And Lena would oblige and pretend to enjoy it, even though she was secretly reluctant. It was always difficult touching someone like that – such disgustingly soft skin! – after so many months at the house with no one else around other than Mother and the staff. Even when she became older and more mature, it never failed to feel challenging.

It also didn't help that the drone tended to hover over Isabella during these sorts of moments, buzzing in her ear in a way that Lena found – well, a bit overbearing. He also often gave Isabella instructions that Lena found painfully obvious, like *Please keep away from the barbed wire.* Of course Isabella was going to stay away from the barbed wire! What did he think she was going to do, dive into it head first? But, like Mother, the drone was only trying to do his job, and that wasn't something Lena could hold against him.

But take how Isabella was never allowed to enter the deepest parts of the river, as the drone consistently assessed that the water wasn't adequately safe. Lena found this a bit much – to travel all the way here, on that long (presumably nauseating) helicopter ride, and then never actually go swimming? She felt this was more about the drone himself being afraid of water, which Mother confirmed: *These military types, Lena – if you ever meet more of them, and I hope to God you never do, you'll see for yourself that there's always something a bit off with them; they all have their neuroses. Some of them can be real sickos. But you can't blame them! They've been through a lot, it's no wonder that they aren't right in the head. They're paranoid, they're bossy, and God forbid you ever contradict them. But they've made a big sacrifice, Lena, a sacrifice for us all, for this country, so they're deserving of our respect. Just do what he says and respect his requests, and whatever you do, don't get on his bad side or create any drama, because he's not going away any time soon and you don't want to cause any problems.*

Mother was right, because Mother was always right about these kinds of things. The world was a complicated place, and Mother understood it much better than she did. But at least when things were normal – when it was just her and Mother and the staff – Lena could go out swimming in the river as far as she wanted. She liked the spot where slimy black fish nibbled her ankles, and the current smacked against rocks. Sometimes the spray hit her own face so hard it felt like a slap.

Isabella was always happy enough with dangling her feet off the dock or playing on the sand. When Isabella was happy, the drone was happy, and when the drone was happy, Lena could relax. He would tell Isabella's parents that Lena was a good caretaker, a nice girl. A good person. That she wasn't an inconvenience, and they should continue letting her stay here at the house, that it was fine to let her go on living here with Mother; she was a big help and wasn't any trouble. What would happen to Lena if she *was* trouble? What would 'Lena being trouble' look like, exactly? It wasn't sensible to think about it too much. Still, before every visit, Mother never failed to issue her standard warning: *Don't forget, Lena, it's very kind of them to let you stay here with me, so let's not cause any drama to make them think otherwise.*

Mother had a great fear of drama. She cautioned against it quite frequently.

By the house the drone was always a bit more relaxed; it was only when they wandered further away, deeper into the jungle, that he became more tense. In the private cove, for example, he would only let Isabella wade in up to her ankles. Lena would show Isabella how to hunt for caterpillars on the underside of leaves, and the drone would tersely interrupt with, *Be careful, they sting.* And when she pointed out logs and explained how to correctly identify a caiman, it was clearly *not* a conversation topic that the drone enjoyed at all. Perhaps Lena wasn't exactly following Mother's advice to avoid drama in these moments, but she couldn't help herself – it was so amusing, the drone's horrified reaction.

And then, in the evenings after the family showered for at least the third time that day, Silvana and Alfonso would prepare wonderful dinners outside, over the barbecue pit and wood stove. Fish stews or grilled meat, depending on what Mother had scheduled and what the helicopters had brought. Lena was especially good at making juices – she consistently got the balance of sugar and fruit exactly right. The family would eat and eat, and drink and drink, until they clutched their ribs and groaned. Lena never ate with them, but Isabella's parents sometimes asked her to attend their arrival and departure meals, which were inevitably celebratory and epic. Fried plantains, rice with shrimp, lobsters with onions, tiny wedges of lime – it could be a bit overwhelming. Overwhelming options, overwhelming amounts. Sometimes Alfonso went so far as to prepare oysters, but he was terrible at shucking them, and as he became older and rustier and generally more confused, they became increasingly rare on the menu. Without the Morels around, Lena was content with fish and rice, beans and potatoes, the occasional chicken soup. Simple food, easy to prepare. Nothing like what they put on for the family.

Lena felt quite tense when eating in front of the family and preferred not to. She worried about dropping grains of rice down her shirt or forgetting to wipe away sauce smeared on her chin. She also worried they'd notice how much she ate. In front of the Morels, it was important to be polite. Mother made her sit through countless lessons about table manners, but it still didn't prevent Lena from getting nervous. She liked having the family come, especially Isabella, but as she grew older, it became harder to adjust to them rather than easier.

'Aren't you darling!' That's what Mrs Morel had said the first time she saw Lena, when she was nine. How anxious Lena had been! Her back pressing against the wall, her hands hot and dry. It had taken all her courage not to slink away, or hide her face against Silvana's cool metal torso. It was only the sound of Mother's voice in her head that kept her in place, albeit with trembling legs: *I'll deal with them, Lena. Just focus on your three main responsibilities. Do you remember what those are?*

Lena, reciting dutifully: *Not call you Mother in front of them. Not cause drama. Be nice and polite, especially to Isabella.*

Exactly. Even still, the windows and doors kept opening and closing at random, betraying Mother's nervousness.

'Absolutely darling,' Mrs Morel repeated. She patted Lena on the cheek a few times. Lena closed her eyes but forced herself to stay put – how strange Mrs Morel's hand felt. Disturbingly warm and sticky. Nothing like Silvana's or Alfonso's. 'She's just as you described her, Jungle House. Very cute, but a little surly. Come closer, Lena, we won't harm you.'

'Yes,' Mother said. 'Lena's services as a local guide, and capacity to provide indigenous knowledge, will enhance Isabella's jungle experience and provide invaluable authenticity to her stay.'

'Wonderful,' Mrs Morel said. Mr Morel wasn't paying attention; he was already walking upstairs, dropping cigar ash on the steps Alfonso had spent all morning carefully sweeping. Isabella had been hiding behind Mrs Morel's leg this entire exchange, which gave Lena a strange feeling. (It was just Isabella at that point; the Morels wouldn't purchase the drone until the following year.) Isabella, wrapping her hand in her mother's. Burying her face in her mother's shirt, occasionally peering out at Lena, crossing her eyes, poking out her tongue when the adults weren't looking. Lena, though, had to stand there alone. Even though she pressed her back against the wall as hard as she could, it felt nothing at all like an embrace. All she had was Mother's voice in her head. And what was Mother saying to her?

Be nice, Lena.

And so, Lena stepped forward. Isabella looked up at her, with a strange look of haughtiness that made Lena bristle. For the briefest of seconds, she pictured herself storming off. But no, that wouldn't do. She had to do as Mother said.

And so, Lena asked, 'Would you like to see the pool?' Extending her hand, just like she'd practised with Silvana and Alfonso. Her fingers were shaking slightly, so, forcefully, consciously, she made them stop.

Isabella snorted. But Mrs Morel gave her a nudge.

'Fine,' Isabella said without smiling. She reached out and took Lena's hand. Lena imagined Mother sighing with relief. The locks of the doors unclicked as Mother relaxed, but nobody apart from Lena noticed.

It was a relief to Lena when at first Isabella's parents basically ignored her. But as she grew older, they began to look at her. To *really* look at her. Like the time Mr Morel asked if she would walk around the table a few times, which she did so obligingly.

'Look,' he said, nudging his wife by the elbow. 'Watch the way she lifts her feet.'

Mrs Morel watched carefully, and made a face that Lena wasn't sure how to interpret. 'Strange!' she said. She made Lena circle the table again before they got distracted by a falling mango, and Lena was then able to slip away quickly and go help Alfonso with the dishes.

She begged Mother later to replay the memory and explain it to her. Mother was usually steadfast in her absolute refusal to show Lena any of her memories, but on this occasion she was surprisingly willing. *I would interpret this as concern, Lena – see the lined forehead? Her mouth is also pulling down but remains shut. If it were disgust, or even fear, the mouth would be slightly open.*

But concern for what, Mother? And why?

It's the way you walk, Lena – you lift your feet too high. You're used to raising them in order to avoid tripping over a root, or sinking in the leaves, or getting tangled in branches. It makes you look strange to them.

It did?

She tried to walk differently after that – tiny, delicate, light steps, like the tinamous when they scurried away with their chicks. But it was hard to maintain, and it didn't take long to become tedious. So she looked strange when she walked – so what? Let her look strange! For the forty-odd weeks of the year that the family weren't present, she could walk however she wanted, and it made no difference to anybody else who lived with her. Mother, Silvana and Alfonso, the pit bull most of all – none of *them* cared.

Still, there was always a part of her that felt a bit embarrassed about it.

Another unfortunate incident was the time with her and Isabella by the pool. Lena was fourteen, and Isabella was twelve. That was the summer Isabella became completely obsessed with sunbathing, which was understandable – she wasn't allowed to go outside City House, not even on the balcony. Lena had just finished swimming laps. Panting hard, she'd collapsed next to Isabella on the same beach towel. It wasn't the kind of position Lena would normally assume – she usually kept more of a respectful distance. But she was exhausted and wanted to rest (as she told Mother later, *I wasn't thinking clearly*). Isabella's eyes were closed, and she made no sign whatsoever of noticing Lena's presence. The drone sat there too, squat and unmoving, absorbing direct sunlight for his battery. It felt nice for Lena to lie there too, soaking up the sun. But then Mrs Morel had come outside to smoke a cigarette and immediately started laughing – a light-hearted, tinkling sound.

'Well, Lena!' she exclaimed. 'Aren't you uppity!'

Isabella opened her eyes immediately and stared at Lena. Her lip curled slightly, as it did when eating something distasteful. For a moment Lena didn't do anything: first came the embarrassment, washing over her body in a wave of goose pimples. Then came the anger, gathering in the back of her throat like bile. In that moment, she wanted nothing more than to give Isabella a good hard smack. Mrs Morel, too. But she could imagine Mother's voice, speaking in her head: *No drama, Lena.* And so Lena quickly shuffled off the towel, so that their buttocks were no longer sharing the same piece of fabric. Playing with Isabella was fine, keeping Isabella company was fine, but there seemed to be a line Mrs Morel didn't want her to cross, and for whatever reason sitting on the same towel as Isabella was exactly that. And then she'd felt the most terrible sense of shame, more soaking and immersive than the pool water could ever be.

Mother never mentioned it. She didn't even reprimand Lena for it later. But the drone – he said something to her afterwards, in that sharp, abrupt way of his, when Isabella had stood up and was shaking the towel out carefully over the patio tiles.

'That wasn't right,' he said. 'What she said to you.' He spoke quietly, like he didn't want to be heard.

'Pardon?' Lena said, startled. It was the first time he'd ever addressed her directly.

But the drone didn't speak further. Instead, he zoomed closer to Isabella as she draped the wet towel over her arm and headed inside. Her wet feet left prints on the tiles that disappeared instantly in the white-hot sun.

So yes, it could be a bit intense and exhausting to deal with the Morels. How loud, how red-faced they could be. They inevitably broke down near the end of their visits and left a full day early. The humidity, the storms, the bugs, the snakes. Mrs Morel would even get frustrated at how often her glasses steamed up. It could be a bit much at times. Lena would end up spending more time in the bathroom than was necessary, or shutting herself in the cupboard with the bleach and buckets and extra dustpans. Silvana and Alfonso would usually be in there as well, seizing the opportunity to recharge at the wall socket (no matter how often they charged, though, it seemed like their batteries could never hold it for long – an early sign of their impending fate). She found it comforting to lean against them, feeling the warmth in their bodies from the charge. Sometimes she even wrapped her arms around their torsos. The same way she clung on to them as a child, letting them drag her from room to room. Closing her eyes. Deep, shaky breaths.

It didn't help that Isabella could be so cutting sometimes, especially as she got older, about how 'primitive' and 'old' Jungle House was, compared to City House. How it pained Lena to hear such pointed remarks! There was that one visit, for example, where Isabella spent the entire time complaining about the lack of external weather control, no artificial climate generator . . . not to mention her subtle critiques about Silvana and Alfonso. *Wow,*

I never knew droids this old still existed! Where did you get them, Mummy – an antique shop?

And then there were Isabella's remarks about Lena herself. 'Why are the pores on your nose so big?' she often asked. 'And the hairs on your chin so dark?'

But still. It was nice seeing them. It was always nice, having them come. Isabella and Lena were so close in age. She and Isabella laughed a lot together. They had a good time.

Isabella's parents, too. Take Lena's party trick with leftover fish, for instance – she could pick the bones cleaner than any of them, and suck out the eyes with gusto. Mr Morel would over-praise her, and Mrs Morel would laugh, and Isabella would groan in overdramatic disgust. 'Come, Lena!' they would call. 'Come do your fish trick!' And Lena would come. The more dramatically she sucked out the eyeballs, the louder they would cheer: *absolutely disgusting!* After dinner, Lena would help Isabella with her bedtime routine – shower, story time, song when Isabella was young; combing her hair and cleaning her biotech-device implant when Isabella was older. In the meantime, Mother would provide Isabella's parents with music or films or simulations to wander through, whatever they might like. Mr Morel preferred to go to bed early – he worked so hard at the base, he liked his time at the house to be restful. But Mrs Morel loved to drink late into the night and admire the sky, the stars, the pock-faced moon most of all.

At night Lena would often be busy getting Isabella settled and tidying up, leaving Mrs Morel to herself. However, there was one incident that occurred during the Morels' last visit. Lena had come into the living room to clean up the remaining evening debris – platters of salted peanuts, glasses of half-melted ice cubes – and Mrs Morel had called her over. 'Come, Lena,' she said. 'Come chat with me for a bit.'

And Lena obliged. Mrs Morel had never before made this kind of request – to speak with Lena alone – so Lena felt it would be rude to refuse. But how would Mother feel, watching Lena and Mrs Morel converse privately? Lena did her best to hide her anxiety – hopefully, Mrs Morel wouldn't notice.

'You're lucky, Lena.' That's what Mrs Morel said, the rapidly melting ice cubes making no sound in her drink as she raised it. 'So lucky to live here. You don't get stars like this back home. Too many lights.' She talked about the greyness of the city – such a contrast to the greenness of the jungle. Since the conclusion of peace negotiations, security in the city had vastly improved. Still, there were memories around every corner: the bombings, the hostages, the violence. 'You've never seen the city, have you, Lena?'

Lena nodded politely. 'That's correct.'

'You'll have to come back with us sometime. It'd be quite the experience for you!'

It was then that Mother interrupted: 'Mrs Morel, there's quite the unique configuration of stars tonight. Would you like to hear about the constellations?' Without waiting for a response, she helpfully projected a replica of the night sky on to the living-room wall, pointing out which star was which, what was a planet as opposed to a satellite. But Mrs Morel seemed unbothered, so Lena gratefully seized the chance to retreat to the kitchen.

'Sorry, Mother,' she said by the sink. She was whispering, but Mother would still be able to hear. In her head, she could imagine Mother's response: *Whatever, Lena. If you want to get all cosy and intimate with Mrs Morel, fine by me. I'm surprised it hasn't happened sooner.* But Mother didn't speak. In that way, Mother's silence in that moment said more than any of her words ever could.

Before the family arrived, Mother always had everything sorted. She'd tell the helicopter to bring liquor and cigarettes, as well as popsicles for the freezer (coconut and lime, Isabella's favourites). She'd make sure Silvana had plenty of freshly caught fish and assess what Alfonso needed to best maintain the property. The house was always well stocked, and apart from local game and vegetables, most essential supplies were delivered by helicopter, the one that brought Isabella and her parents from the base. Of course, if an emergency were to happen, Lena could always travel by canoe to the village, which apparently had a store . . . but there'd never been any need for that. No reason to go, no need to bother. Mother and the helicopter always got along surprisingly well – it was so hard to predict at times, who Mother would judge as useless and who she'd assess as helpful! *To be honest, Lena, he's a bit of a gossip – some of the things he tells me, I wish I didn't know. But he's always on time, and consistency is something to be valued, believe me.*

Like the helicopter, Mother also loved to gossip, particularly about the satellites and their countless dramas. The treacherous one who abruptly left his orbit and headed to Mars; the weirdo who'd been obsessively watching the same glacier for years; the drama queens who hadn't spoken in a decade due to a misfired missile. But that wasn't the kind of thing Mother ever did with the Morels present. Lena had noticed that Mother didn't want the Morels to know how often she and the satellites gossiped. It would cause drama.

What else did the Morels like to do on their visits? They used to hike out to see the waterfall, but then one summer Mother informed them this was unwise, due to rumoured rebel presence, and they never went again. Lena still went on her own, but obviously that was different. The Morels weren't as familiar with the area as Lena, and it would be inadvisable for them to assume any unnecessary risks.

Good times. They'd had some good times. All those years together, and all that fun.

Things were different now, of course.

But Lena still held a hard kernel of belief within her. Like a pebble swallowed by one of the parrots she raised as a child. The Morels would return. Yes, it might take years – but they'd stayed away for long periods of time before, hadn't they? Lena herself hadn't even met them in person until she'd turned nine! And it's already been over a year since they last came. Since it happened.

A year was probably not quite enough time for them to recover, to be fair.

But at some point, the Morels would come back. Life was surely carrying on for them in the city, as it went on for Lena in the jungle. Mr Morel was likely extraordinarily busy in his national security job, and Mrs Morel was probably occupied with her painting and her charity work. They *would* come back eventually, and some sense of normality and routine would be restored. It would.

The cut-off satellite connection, though. That . . . wasn't a good sign. Neither were the binoculars by the house. There was no way around it. They were problems. It was drama.

And then there was the matter of the drone.

That was drama, too.

'Horrible,' Mother sighs. 'Maybe it's for the best we can't send the Morels messages anymore. They'd probably ask the army to fire-bomb the entire area, me included. Not a bad idea, quite frankly.'

Lena lowers the binoculars into her lap. She's sitting on the couch in the living room, so that she and Mother can converse more easily. It doesn't technically make a difference – Mother could hear perfectly well if she stayed outside on the patio – but she knows it makes Mother feel better, having her close, inside. Neither of them acknowledges it's been a month since Lena was last here.

'Oh, Lena,' Mother says. 'You should probably just set fire to the whole damn place yourself and be done with it. Don't leave anything for them to raid; don't let yourself get taken hostage. If the flames burn high enough, the army will come to investigate. Hopefully.' She pauses. 'I wonder how long it'll take for me to melt. I can withstand a temperature of a thousand degrees. Supposedly.' She rapidly flicks the light switch up and down, a long-time anxious habit she only ever does around Lena. But the bulbs don't turn on – how long have they been burnt out? Is the power out completely? Has Mother been sitting in the dark this whole time, with Lena away in the hut?

'Please don't be crazy.' She hates it when Mother gets like this.

'It's true, though. But even without the solar panels, I can survive up to a hundred years. What a fun life that'll be! No one but me for company. A brain in a box.'

'Well, it's never going to happen, so there's no point in worrying about it.'

'But whatever you do, Lena, don't throw any of my eyes in the river. I'll just float forever and spend the rest of my godforsaken life watching algae grow. If I'm especially unlucky a caiman will swallow me. Can you imagine a worse fate?' Mother cackles.

'Mother!'

After a month away, it's easy to note what's fallen into disrepair. Dust on the ceramic figures, spiderwebs on the bookshelves. And there, in the upper left corner of the ceiling – is that another termites' nest? Have they moved in that quickly? The couch feels damp beneath Lena's trousers, there's a strong smell in the room reminiscent of mushrooms – Mother's worst nightmare! – and even the curtains are speckled with black spots of mould.

How disarming it is – to see how quickly it can all change.

Neglectful, she thinks. I've been neglectful.

'You're staying here, then,' Mother says. She doesn't even phrase it as a question.

Lena doesn't respond.

'With rebels this close, you can't be out there in the hut, all by yourself—'

Lena shuffles around on the couch. The smell of mushrooms grows even stronger.

'Lena,' Mother says, and this time her voice is measured and calm. 'This is not a risk to be underestimated. I am not in any way exaggerating. The rebels will take you, Lena. *Kidnap* you. They'll make you march up into the mountains. They'll make you do drills. You'll be forced to wear their uniform, and you'll never see me again. They'll rape you. They'll enslave you. If you get pregnant, they'll make you abandon your baby. They'll—'

'I *know*!' Lena says. 'I know, I know, I know. Fine. Yes. Okay. I'll move back into the house.'

'Good,' Mother says. 'It's the most sensible decision.'

'Uh-huh.'

'It really isn't safe—'

'You already made that perfectly clear, thanks.'

'Well,' Mother says. Her voice is still very calm. 'That's settled, then.'

Lena rubs a finger over the binoculars' lenses. 'You really didn't see?' she asks, even though she knows the question is pointless.

'No, Lena. During my spells, it's hopeless, I don't see or notice a thing. I know, I know, I should be put directly in the trash, I should be smashed to bits, I'm not even worth recycling . . .'

Off she goes. Lena doesn't bother interrupting.

It's a tricky thought to have. But she goes ahead and has it anyway. Sometimes . . . it seems like Mother's spells conveniently occur during moments of great drama. When there's something truly vital to be seen.

It's a thought Lena's had before. But it's not something she would ever dare express aloud.

If one of Mother's main jobs is to protect the property – to see, to watch – then what did it mean that Mother kept failing to do exactly that?

Mother, failing. Mother, old.

Lena raises the binoculars to her eyes once more. How heavy they are! And in surprisingly good condition – a few scratches, but otherwise fine. They're considerably dirty, as though recently dug up. The view through them is blurry. She rotates here, fiddles there, twists the ridged wheel back and forth. But her surroundings still don't come into view – they remain murky, indistinct.

Where did they come from? Could it have been a local from the village, rather than a rebel? But the closest village is well over three days' walk away. Why would they approach the property? Why would a villager own such equipment?

The drone – perhaps he witnessed something. Maybe the drone can help. Highly unlikely, but still possible. In order to find out, though, she'll have to ask him herself.

She can help, too. She'll put things right again, back to how they were before. Yes, she and Mother had their argument, their little spat, but it was fine now. Things were fine. She was here. She was back. She and Mother, together again, just like normal.

And with rebels potentially in the area, it *did* make sense for

Lena to move back into the house. What happened with the pit bull – it was behind them now.

Poor Mother – all alone this past month. And with the house in such a state!

I'll do the curtains first, she thinks. Those are always hardest. The bulbs are dead, but she can check storage for spares. And if the power is out, she can turn on the generator. Mother will hate wasting gas, but surely it'll be fine to have it on briefly. The swimming pool is a complete disaster – she should have followed Mother's advice and never emptied it in the first place – but she could clean it up. She could make things normal again – make things right.

'Lena,' Mother says, 'you're daydreaming again. Where are you? Where did you go?'

'Here, Mother,' she says. 'I haven't gone anywhere – I'm right here.'

She puts her hand on the wall. When she was a child, she would do silly things like this all the time – kiss the doorknob, or hug a drainpipe – in the misguided, childish belief that it was the kind of thing that Mother could feel. But she's a grown woman now, not a child, and Mother herself is much older than the family ever expected her to be or become.

'Oh!' Mother says, in a little cry that is also a sigh. 'That feels nice, Lena.'

They both know she's lying. Her hand stays on the wall.

Chapter Three

OUT OF ALL THE ROOMS in the house, Lena attends to Isabella's the most. Yes, the master bedroom is in desperate need of a vacuuming, not to mention a massive dose of insecticide for the never-ending ant invasion. Yes, walking barefoot anywhere on the floor will inevitably result in having to wipe the bottom of her foot off on her calf. And yes, along with the possums, there's probably a bat colony in the chimney – the fact that Mother hasn't bitched about them yet is truly a miracle.

She has no interest whatsoever in checking her own room – the smallest one in the house besides Mother's. A scratched-up wooden door down the hallway, past the kitchen. She turns the knob experimentally but of course it doesn't open; she'd have to shove down hard with all her strength. In there are Silvana and Alfonso. Stored away, sitting on her bed. *Surely there's a better place to keep them, Lena. Put them in the shed, for God's sake. It makes no sense, kicking yourself out of your own room.* But Lena had insisted: it was the only place that felt right. Silvana and Alfonso didn't belong in storage with the barbecue grill, or the broken dryer, or the microwave with the faulty light. They deserved their privacy, their peace. But right now, it's not a scene she's willing to confront, not yet. Still, she briefly touches her forehead against the wooden surface, before turning away.

The trip up the stairs – dead roaches, dried-up moths, fearful lizards skittering away – is enough to drench Lena with even more guilt. She's really let things slide – one month away, and look. Look! But she's back now. Isn't that what counts?

Just like her own door, the one to Isabella's bedroom tends to stick. All wood throughout the house has warped due to years of intense humidity and moisture, so there's no chance of ever sneaking into any of the bedrooms without making a loud noise – not that there'd ever be any reason to sneak, of course. As usual, she has to put her shoulder to the door in order to push it open, but then enters as quietly as she can.

In the brief second before it blinks out completely – before he shuts it off – she can see it. Briefly, but she sees.

Isabella, standing there in her pink rain jacket. Lena's stomach twists at the sight. Isabella's arm points upwards; her lips move, she's smiling. And then she's gone.

'Good afternoon!' Lena calls out with forced brightness. But as expected, there's no reply.

In contrast to the rest of the house, Isabella's bedroom is quite bare. There are two hooks on the wall for Isabella's rain jackets (only the purple one is left, the one she claimed leaked and never used). There's a chest of drawers with its too cluttered surface: brushes, creams, collected seed pods. Battered clay animals she and Lena made as children – it's hard to tell now what they're meant to represent. One is either a cow or a puma, but another is reassuringly identifiable as a toucan, thanks to the beak. There's a closet and the chair. A bed and the air-conditioning unit. The windowsill is lined with pebbles and shells collected from the river. And there's the window, and its balcony view.

Lena inspects the room, but apart from the dead flies and streaks of dust – easily amended with a damp cloth and furniture polish – everything is acceptable. Daring to hope, she looks up to the rafters. She then looks at the mattress, but there's no lump under the single thin sheet, no hunched, trembling shape. The woollen blankets were folded up long ago, as they are at the end of every rainy season, stored away in the wooden trunk in the hallway. Stored by Lena. Most of what's been done here is Lena's work.

She sighs. It was silly of her to think it would be otherwise – that the situation would be different. Every time she visits, it's the same. She carefully sets the binoculars on the thin flat pillows, before getting down on her knees and looking under the bed.

'Good afternoon,' she repeats, keeping her voice low. 'I hope you're doing well.'

The drone doesn't reply.

'I'm sorry to disturb you,' she says, a bit louder this time, even though it shouldn't make a difference; his hearing is vastly superior to Mother's. Vision, too.

The drone turns in her direction, a slow, weary shuffle. Tiny dust motes float in the air, which Lena notes with dismay. 'Oh,' he says flatly, as if just noticing her presence. 'Hello, Lena.'

He's in his usual spot: as far under the bed as it's possible to get, close to the wall. Surrounded by wisps of hair, mouse droppings (oh *no*), a deflated rubber ball, an ancient headless doll with teeth marks. Was that the one they used to call Crystal, the one she and Isabella had tea parties with? A stool with a missing leg, a sun-bleached teacup, a ratty towel covered in dark yellow stains. This and that. Things Isabella no longer wanted and could no longer use. General mess.

Every time she enters the room, despite her best instincts, it's always there: the tiniest sliver of hope that he might – you know. Be feeling a bit better about things. A bit more willing to move on with life, accept the situation. The Morels had left him here; they hadn't taken him back to the city. Along with Lena, he'd been interrogated extensively by the search parties (unlike Lena, his data was downloaded, scanned, and stored accordingly). Even after the search parties concluded that there was nothing more that could be done, the Morels hadn't summoned the drone to return. It was shocking they hadn't had him decommissioned – *thrown on the scrap heap,* as Mother would say. But their apparent indifference to him disturbed Lena greatly. Why had they left him running, despite having failed at his one essential duty – and failed so spectacularly, at that? Perhaps the Morels still needed him around for one reason or another; perhaps they had future plans for him – though what these might be, Lena couldn't possibly say.

What did Mother think of the drone? Lena has never heard them address each other, not aloud – if they do speak, it's the same way that Mother speaks with the satellites. She rarely mentions him, apart from a few curt asides practically interchangeable from similar comments she's made about the helicopters and City House and Mountain House and God knows who else, whoever has most recently got on Mother's nerves. Comments of a similar nature, all blurring together in Lena's head: *He thinks he's so much better than me, Lena, just because he can fly around. Big freaking deal. Whoop-de-doo for him. Trust me, dealing with someone with that kind of personality is a complete waste of time.* Mother often used the exact same phrases when discussing the major irritants in her life – sometimes when she was off on her rants, Lena felt like mouthing along, reciting the lines with her. But she'd never dare.

Lena has always suspected that Mother is jealous of the drone. The drone can go places; can see things Mother never will. The drone could be close to Isabella – close to Lena, too – in a way that Mother can't.

Today doesn't seem to be one of his good days.

'So . . .' she says. Addressing the drone by name – the one that Isabella selected, and that only Isabella ever used – would be an insane invasion of privacy, unbelievably rude. It was only ever Isabella who addressed him directly. But it makes speaking to him now a bit awkward. 'Are you charging?'

It's a foolish question, considering there's no sunlight under the bed. But he still answers politely. 'Not at the minute, no,' he says. 'To be honest, that's been a bit of a struggle lately.' He pauses, as if not wanting to elaborate. 'I was at the window earlier, though.'

'You were?'

He'd been at the window the last time she visited. He'd shown her the macaws. He must hear it now when she speaks, that high-pitched note of hope. He looks at her directly.

'Yes,' he says. 'I was watching the juveniles. It's incredible how fast they grow.'

'Oh!' She wiggles forward a bit – encouragingly, the drone doesn't shrink away. She rests her chin on her arms. 'Have you been watching them long? Did you see them fledge?'

'I did indeed.'

His voice is deep and masculine, but there's a tentativeness to it – Mother is far more forceful and authoritative. How formal he is! It makes her stiff and polite in turn, like an insect that needs to imitate the branch it's sitting on in order to survive. Mother's moods are easier to deal with; at least Lena is used to them. The flat melancholy of the drone, and the way it rises off him like early morning mist on the river – that's what she doesn't want to touch.

'I can show you,' he says. 'If you'd like.'

He did this the last time she visited too, with the macaws. This is what she's been hoping for all along. Mother is unbelievably greedy with her memories, so stand-offish and protective. Apart from exceptional occasions – like showing Lena how funnily she walked, for instance – she never replays them for Lena, ever. Even though she has so many more than the drone.

Silvana and Alfonso have memories, too. Unlike Mother and the drone, who require specific equipment for memory extraction, Lena can access Silvana and Alfonso's memories herself, via a button on the back of their skulls. Theoretically, at any time, Lena could just press this button and watch everything Silvana and Alfonso have ever recorded. Their whole lives, every moment. But Mother has never allowed it, will never allow it. It might be Mother's number one rule, out of the many that she has. *Let me have my privacy, Lena – don't be disgusting. How would you feel if someone opened up* your *skull and had a look inside?*

The drone's willingness to share is therefore a delightful contrast. 'That would be *wonderful*,' she says, trying hard not to sound eager, and failing.

The drone hums. He shudders. He jolts upwards, banging against the metal rods of the bed frame. Lena holds her breath.

The hologram is playing behind her, so she has to twist around to watch. It's wavery, flickering in and out like all of the drone's memories.

Two speckled juvenile hawks sit in the nest. They flap their wings, open their beaks, but there's no sound. She watches as one of them stands tentatively on the nest's edge, spreading its wings. Flap, flap, flap. And then the leap, the launch into space. It looks more like falling than flying.

'It was the female, then,' she says. 'The one that went first.'

'I'm not sure, Lena; you would know better than me.'

He rewinds the memory so she can watch it again. Flap, flap, flap. She watches carefully.

'It's hard to tell,' she admits. 'It looks bigger, but I don't know if that's just because of the angle, from where you were sitting.'

'If you think it was female, you should trust your judgement. You watch them every year, don't you?'

'I do.'

'Then you know what you're talking about. Out of all of us here, you know the jungle best.'

The back of her head is to him, so he can't see her smile. Being praised feels nice, if a bit strange.

He keeps rewinding. The juveniles go to sleep, wake up. They cry, call, tear apart meat brought to them by their parents, who flicker in and out of the recording in quick, indistinct blurs. What a shame the images aren't sharper, more precise, but he is who he is; like Mother, he isn't young anymore.

'Wow!' she says, surprised by the force of her happiness. 'You were watching them for ages!'

He doesn't answer, he keeps going. The brown juvenile feathers are sucked back into their bodies and turn into white fluff. The birds shrink in size, their wings diminish. They become smaller, cuter, fluffier. She can't help it; she's holding her breath again. It's so pleasurable to see them up close. But then they disappear, blink out of existence, and all she's left with is the dirt-specked wall, and a centipede crawling across it.

'That's it,' the drone says. 'That's as far back as I saw. Sorry. You probably would have liked to see them hatch, I guess. Or crawl back into the egg, I mean. Ha ha.' Unlike Mother, his laugh is self-conscious, more of a recitation.

'Oh, no!' She twists around so that they're facing again. 'That was wonderful. I love that you watched them so long.'

'They're beautiful, aren't they?'

'Yes . . .' She hesitates. 'What do you like about them most?'

Her voice is still stiff – you'd think that, after all these years, she'd be more proficient at talking to someone who isn't Mother. But it still feels odd: here's another mind before her, a completely different being. Is this another reason Lena likes to visit him? A chance to talk to someone different. Someone new.

Somebody who's not Mother.

But the drone replies without missing a beat, like there was nothing awkward whatsoever about Lena's delivery. 'I admire how they move. Especially when they fly.'

Lena can't help but laugh. 'You mean when they fly like you?'

'No, not like me at all – they're free.' The drone says this like it's the most obvious thing in the world. It makes Lena look down at the floor.

She's heard from Mother about other types of drones – the ones with chips implanted that make them self-destruct, if they wander too far from the client they've been assigned to protect. That obviously isn't the case with this drone – he's still here, and Isabella isn't.

'Well, anyway . . . thanks for showing me.' She hesitates again, but goes ahead and says it recklessly, like when she goes outside at night in bare feet, even though that's when the fer de lances are out and about. 'Anton,' she says. 'Thank you, Anton.'

For a second, he doesn't say anything. For a second, she thinks it's okay. But then he turns around so quickly he bangs against the metal rods of the bed again, louder than before. If somebody else was in the house, somebody besides Mother, they might look up towards the ceiling and wonder *What on earth was that?* But it's just the drone, turning around so that his back is to Lena, and that's how she knows that she's gone ahead and ruined it, and any hope she may have had of asking him about the binoculars is gone. If he was watching the property, if there was any chance he may have seen someone – an intruder, a trespasser that Mother somehow missed during her spell – now is not the time to ask. Using his name – the one that no one other than Isabella ever used – has brought the past into the room, the past he doesn't want to look at, the past he can apparently only ever confront when he's alone, playing and replaying his memories (his version of them), flickering on the wall. There's nothing left to do but pick up the binoculars from the bed and return downstairs, and the drone will presumably go on looking at the wall, staring at it in the same way he's been staring for months and months, and if he ever wants to go back to this moment and revisit it, this is what he will have, this is what it will look like, the exact same view over and over, unchanged.

The drone spoke to Lena once more in the summer of the 'uppity' incident. It happened a few days afterwards, in Isabella's bedroom. In those days Isabella often had nightmares and would ask Lena to stay with her until she fell asleep. Lena never refused anything Isabella asked.

She'd become used to the family by then, even if not necessarily comfortable. Her first summer of being around them had been an adjustment, so different from everything and anything else she had ever experienced at that point in her life. The noise of the Morels! That was what stunned her the most – new voices in the house. Voices that weren't Mother or the jungle. And the physicality of them – the smudges left behind on glasses. The sweat-darkened clothes, the musky scents, so different from Lena's – sharper somehow, and sourer. They all showered several times a day, but it didn't help.

On this particular evening, Mother was reciting the tale of *Sleeping Beauty*. Even at age twelve, Isabella still requested bedtime stories, and so Mother persisted with the nightly ritual. In Lena's opinion, Mother was terrible at storytelling, her delivery inevitably flat and recitative. She was also constantly interrupting herself with comments like, *Of course, all of this is incredibly unrealistic, verging on absurd . . .*

Mother wasn't doing too badly this time, though. She had got as far as the finger pricking on the spindle – the spark of blood, Sleeping Beauty letting out a cry – when Isabella interrupted.

'Stop, Jungle House,' she said. 'I want Lena to do it. I want a story about the jungle. About *here.*'

'Of course!' Mother said. 'My apologies, Isabella. Lena, go ahead.'

But Lena hesitated. Picking at the tasselled edges of the blanket, she said, 'Isabella, bedtime stories have always been Jungle House's job.' It always felt incredibly unnatural, referring to Mother as 'Jungle House', but that was what Mother instructed her to do, so that's what she did. *It's better if they don't know how close we are, Lena. It won't result in anything good.*

And Lena had agreed, because Mother knew so much more about these things than she ever could.

'Jungle House sucks,' Isabella said. 'I want to hear from you.' She folded her hands expectantly on top of the blankets, a gesture remarkably reminiscent of Mrs Morel's when she was waiting to be served her nightly gin and tonic.

'Go ahead, Lena,' Mother said, in a tone that meant: *Let's keep Isabella happy.*

And so Lena ended up telling some ridiculous tale, invented on the spot: an anteater who struck a secret deal with the ants to live in harmony; moths who teamed up with butterflies; a dolphin and otter who became best friends. Cute stories, cosy stories, ones that made the jungle seem safe and appealing, in a way that Lena instinctively sensed Isabella would enjoy. 'Could I see a dolphin?' Isabella asked, and Lena was forced to explain that, no, like the jaguars, the dolphins were gone, they'd been gone for generations, they weren't coming back.

It was hard telling Isabella stories because, unlike with Mother, she kept interrupting with random questions. 'Lena,' she said, right in the middle of an overtly complicated tale about the secret society of tree rats, 'are there piranhas in the river?'

'No,' Lena said instantly, happy to be distracted – it was a story she'd been fumbling with for ages (why on earth had she made the tree rats team up with the stick insects?). 'You don't have to worry

40

about that, Isabella, you'll never find them here.' She explained that piranhas were only a threat in murky, stagnant water. In the gorge – the only place in the river where Isabella was permitted to wade – the river tumbled over the rocks, and the water that collected in the naturally formed cove was clear and calm; there was no place for them to gather.

'There're snakes, though,' Isabella said when Lena finished. 'Like in my nightmares.'

'That's true,' Lena said. She knew all about Isabella's nightmares: snakes in the bedroom, snakes in her hair. Mrs Morel was also terrified of snakes – she never left the house at night, not even in boots. Sitting by the pool was as far out as she was willing to venture; none of the Morels ever roamed beyond the property at night. In contrast, Lena had gone on many a night walk, and had handled many a snake. Mainly the brown ones that were easy to mistake for branches, but the occasional fluorescent green one too. Not something the family needed to know, though. Lena would hate for them to find her strange.

'There are no snakes in the house,' Lena said, the same phrase Mother always used. 'They can't get in here. Mo— Jungle House won't let them.'

Isabella continued as if she hadn't listened. 'There's also bats that suck your blood,' she said. 'There's leeches, and poison frogs.' She paused. 'And rebels.'

Yes, Lena said. But Isabella didn't need to worry about any of that. Mother kept the windows shut so that bats couldn't get in. Lena knew which leech-dwelling spots in the river to avoid. And Mother wouldn't let any rebels get near. Not now. Not ever. No rebels could even come close to the property; it simply wasn't possible. Mother would never permit it. (It was *especially* important to never mention Mother's spells during this kind of discussion.) In addition to that, in the unlikely scenario that someone *did* come close enough, the drone would never let anyone hurt her. Not now. Not ever.

'Uh-huh,' Isabella said, sounding dubious. 'Jungle House is getting old, though . . .'

Mother couldn't respond to this, of course.

'Isabella!' Lena said, impulsively inventing a random anecdote in a frantic attempt to distract, 'don't you remember last year when you got a leech between your toes, and I pulled it off, and it stretched out really, really far and left a tiny pinprick of blood behind, but you were really brave and tough and didn't scream, not even once?'

'That really happened?' Isabella said incredulously.

Lena bit her lip and nodded.

'Anton, is that true?'

Lena shifted around uncomfortably. How stupid of her, inventing a story like that – she'd spoken quickly without thinking, and was now getting called out on it. Isabella was surely going to be upset.

In the rafters above, in his typical vantage point, the drone made a soft purring sound Lena had never heard before. 'Yes,' he said, 'it's true. That's exactly what happened.'

Lena glanced up at him. But he didn't look back.

'However,' he continued, 'I don't think it's appropriate to be reliving that kind of moment at this time of night. Night-time is for getting calm and comfortable, and ready for sleep.'

'Well, I want to see it,' Isabella said. 'Because I don't remember that happening at all. Jungle House, did you see?'

'I didn't,' Mother said. 'I can't see down to the gorge. The perimeter of my vision is contained to the house, the pool, and—'

'Okay, shut up,' Isabella said. 'Lena, show me.'

Lena was forced to explain that she couldn't. She didn't have the same capacity as Mother, the drone and the droids. 'I'm like you,' Lena said. 'The things I see and remember, they stay here –' she tapped her skull – 'no one can ever see them but me.'

If Isabella was embarrassed by such an obvious mistake, she didn't show it. Instead she shifted her head to a cooler part of the pillow. 'Anton, I want to see it.'

Lena's hands were clutching the blanket far too tight. She forced herself to relax before Isabella noticed.

'Not now, Isabella,' the drone said. 'Lena, I apologise for the inconvenience, but could you excuse us?'

'Of course,' Lena said.

It was just as impossible to shut the door without making a noise as it was to open it. She should have gone down the stairs right away, but she couldn't resist, standing as close to the wood as she dared. *But why, if* . . . Isabella was saying. The drone interrupted, speaking quickly. His tone was urgent, but his voice was too low to make out.

It was pure luck that she'd already moved away from the door when the drone poked it open, nearly banging her elbow. 'Lena!' he whispered. 'Wait!'

She froze. He moved close to her ear, presumably so that he could continue speaking quietly. Even though they weren't touching, she could feel the warmth from his battery humming against her neck.

'Thank you for that,' he said, still whispering. 'I told her it was too late at night to replay it – that the visual stimulation would disrupt her circadian rhythm. She's sulking, but it's fine – she'll forget all about it by morning.'

'Mm,' Lena mumbled. She was far too bewildered to say more. Wasn't it transgressive for the drone, talking to her in private like this? Isabella's personal drone? She wanted to inch away but didn't want to be rude. As ever, she could sense Mother's attention on her, like invisible static in the air. Always there. Always watching.

'She doesn't know I can lie,' the drone said. His voice was flat. 'None of them do.'

To this, Lena had no response. Behind the door, Isabella called out: 'Anton? Why are you talking to Lena?'

He zipped back inside immediately. It was Lena who had to step forward and shut the door, pulling hard so that it closed completely.

That was it – the second time she and the drone ever spoke.

She never found out why the drone lied like that, pretending that Lena's story was true – Isabella and the leeches; her brave, untroubled reaction. A story Lena had made up on the spot. It had made Isabella look brave, though, and was meant to comfort her. Perhaps that's what he'd found appealing.

Isabella's favourite story of all, though – the one she asked Lena to tell again and again – was the one about Lena herself. *Tell me, Lena,* Isabella would say. *Tell me about you. How you came here.* And Lena would oblige. She'd tell Isabella all about it, in a soothing, lulling tone. How she was an orphaned girl from the local village, who'd paddled her leaky canoe upstream. This was in the days before the family had the fence extended to cross the water towards the opposite bank. Lena had walked up to Jungle House, knocking on the door and asking for work. She'd wanted employment, an honest job, and a safe place to live. Never mind that the family had never paid Lena a salary, had never even mentioned it to her – presumably they assumed that being allowed to stay at the house was reimbursement enough. Isabella didn't know that, though. But then again, Isabella preferred asking questions about Lena's past rather than her present. *Tell me about the village,* Isabella said. *What was it like to grow up there?* And Lena would tell her, inventing specific details as she went along, careful to keep them consistent to make it more believable. The smoke-filled huts, the fishing expeditions, the pet monkeys that village children carried on their shoulders (Isabella found this detail especially charming). *You didn't have any parents,* Isabella said. *You didn't have any family or anyone that loved you or wanted you around. But then you heard all about a house in the jungle. A talking house, a magical house. Owned by a nice family, a kind family, and you thought that sounded like a really good place, a safe place to grow up. You came here all by yourself even though you were so young. It was a scary journey, but you were tough, you survived. And then you liked it here so much,* Isabella said, *that you didn't want to leave. You couldn't bear the thought of being anywhere else but here.*

Yes, Lena would say when Isabella finished. *That's right.* And the whole time, the drone stayed perched overhead in the rafters, listening.

It was a lie Mother herself had instructed Lena to tell. A lie Lena has been telling her whole life.

The third time she and the drone addressed each other was a year ago – the last Christmas visit. The family was meant to stay until mid-January, but the rain never stopped once in that first week. Trees fell, branches whipped across windows, and every morning Lena helped Silvana and Alfonso sweep away layers of sodden, matted leaves off the balcony. Even Lena herself felt a bit reproachful – couldn't the sky and river calm down, just a bit? Why did they have to be so worked up when the family was here; couldn't they relax? Perhaps Isabella had a point after all, about getting an artificial climate generator installed . . . But would it even be capable of surviving this sort of wind? Truly, there was so much about the jungle and the area in general that made it unconducive for Mother and the staff: the humidity, the torrential rainfalls, the sporadic sunlight. *I wasn't meant for a place like this*, Mother often complained. *Especially at my age. God knows why I'm still around; it's an absolute miracle my battery hasn't rotted into mush. I don't know what that proves about me, but it proves . . . something! I'm not totally useless yet.*

As a result of the never-ending storm, Mother was in a state of constant tension. She'd been acting faulty since the family arrived: playing music when none was requested, forgetting to turn on lights, answering in a different room than the one they were standing in, opening and shutting doors sporadically. Even Mrs Morel got uncharacteristically irritated. 'Okay, Jungle House, STOP,' she shouted at one point, when Mother was delving into a long speech about wind patterns, when all Mrs Morel had asked for was the temperature. It was terrible for Lena's nerves: the last thing they needed was for the Morels to think there was something wrong with Mother.

Mr Morel had left abruptly on the second day of the holiday, right before the weather worsened. He travelled via helicopter as usual, citing work commitments. There was trouble back at the military base: the presidential election with that awful ex-rebel candidate was looming on the horizon; the protests by those annoying university students hadn't stopped. Mrs Morel stayed behind but kept to herself, spending hours at her studio painting watercolours of the river or sky (it was hard for Lena to tell the difference, and she never dared ask). Lena was nineteen but being around Mrs Morel still made her feel uncomfortable, and ever since their conversation a few days earlier in the living room – *You'll have to come back with us sometime. It'd be quite the experience for you!* – Lena had been doing her best to avoid her.

And Isabella? Isabella had done poorly in her exams and was in a horrible mood. She'd spent most of her time so far in bed on her biotech-device implant, sending the drone to fetch banana-coconut smoothies, which Lena always insisted on making herself, as at the time Silvana wasn't doing so well. The droids had been slowly deteriorating for years, becoming less and less capable, and Lena was desperate for the Morels not to notice.

By the sixth day of the Morels' visit, the rain finally stopped mid-morning. With encouragement from Lena – and a subtle dose of bullying and teasing – Isabella agreed to head down to the leisure area. Isabella stayed on the dock with the drone as she always did, but cheered Lena on as she swam out as far and as fast as she could.

'Well done!' Isabella said when Lena returned, dripping and panting. 'You beat your previous time!' Then they both lay on their backs on the wooden boards, Lena looking up at the sky while Isabella spent time on her device. It had been implanted into her forearm, the usual site. The skin around it was looking particularly swollen and inflamed that day. There were even cracked yellow scabs forming. Lena would have to fetch the tube from the medicine cabinet and start reapplying it at night, until the area improved.

'What are those?' Lena asked, pointing. She didn't mean the device-implant scabs. She meant the bruises on Isabella's inner thighs: purple splotches, with faint tones of yellow. Quite a lot of them too.

But Isabella instantly snapped her legs shut, closing them tightly. 'From the helicopter ride,' Isabella said, a bit too brightly. Nearby, the drone stirred slightly.

She's lying, Lena thought. She doesn't want me to know where they came from. But Lena let the subject drop.

Once the sun became unbearable, Lena took them on a walk down her favourite trail: the path that ran parallel to the leafcutter ants, past the hole where the purple-spotted tarantula lived. Isabella let Lena see the jungle afresh, with new eyes. 'What was *that*?' Isabella often said, halting in her tracks, and it was only then Lena would notice the ever-present sounds around them. The shrilling, the clicking, the rustling, the whining. And growling – yes, there was often growling. 'Oh, God,' Isabella moaned with mocking despair, 'a jaguar?' and Lena reassured her that, no, like the dolphins, the jaguars had been gone for generations; it was probably just a toad. 'No way,' Isabella said. 'Nuh-uh. No toad can make that kind of sound. Absolutely not.'

Absolutely yes, Lena promised. When Isabella swiped away the drops of moisture running down her arm, Lena would suddenly realise how damp everything was. When Isabella furiously pulled at her pink rain jacket, trying to flap it up and down, it was only then Lena became aware of how tightly her own clothing clung to her. And it was only when Isabella wrinkled her nose that the smells would hit Lena too: the mustiness of wood, the sweet decay of plants, the bitter stench of a stink bug. 'Ah!' Isabella cried when bees got tangled in her ponytail, and Lena combed them out with her fingers, reassuring her they were the stingless kind, perfectly harmless; the worst they could do was hang from her hair. There really *were* a lot of insects around, weren't there? Isabella slapped her arms, waved away flies, flicked off a grasshopper clinging to her shirt. To her credit, Isabella didn't complain like when she was younger, and when she did, it was in a high-pitched voice of amusement that she didn't use for anyone else other than Lena. This was part of their dynamic and had been for as long as Lena could remember – Lena was the one who knew the jungle and the property, and Isabella was the outsider, the one who found it shocking when butterflies landed on her arm to sip at her sweat. They love disgusting things, Lena told her, especially blood. Isabella groaned, and they both laughed.

Normally they turned back when they got to the fence. That time, though – the last time – Isabella stood before it for what felt like an uncomfortably long while, inspecting the stakes. It was a simple fence of barbed wire, looped closely together. The stakes had been pounded into the ground generations ago, long before Mother arrived. Perhaps by Henry, Isabella's grandfather. Or maybe even by the Austrian ancestor himself. Lena would have to ask Mother later, to be sure.

'Please keep away from the barbed wire,' the drone said, hovering by Isabella's ear. It annoyed Lena how he always positioned himself slightly ahead of them – she often had to speed up to pass him. After all, she was the one who knew the property best, so why should he lead the way? Eventually, the drone landed on a branch, where he was immediately attacked by botflies, who always found him curious. Lena presumed this branch was the place that gave him the best possible vantage point, so that he could respond efficiently to any possible threat. But there was nobody around but Lena. And Lena wasn't a threat, she was just herself.

The section of jungle on the other side of the fence always seemed different to Lena – darker, denser. Lena knew the jungle on *this* side of the property like the palm of her hand – the trees, the paths, the winding river – but she'd never been on the other side of the fence.

Not at that point, anyway.

In that moment, when Isabella reached out to the wire as if to touch it, Lena spoke right away, interrupting the drone mid-sentence. 'Don't—' he was saying, when Lena cut in.

'It's not electric,' Lena said, 'and Mo— Jungle House has no access to it. But I wouldn't touch it if I were you.'

Isabella promptly dropped her arm back down to her side. She kept looking at the fence. 'No alarms,' she said in that dry, amused voice of hers. 'Or lights.'

Lena took this as an implicit comparison to City House, back at the base, and therefore a critique of Mother's security enforcement. She accepted it silently, grateful that Mother wasn't there to hear it directly – she'd have sulked about it for days, or gone on a rant: *If increased security at the fence is so important to them, then why not invest in it? What am I supposed to do, Lena, when it's just me here, all by myself? Nobody understands the kind of stress I'm under, nobody understands the kinds of challenges I have to face – all of the pressure, it's on me, me, me . . .*

'Couldn't you just lift it up?' Isabella asked. 'And crawl under?'

'Theoretically, yeah,' Lena said. 'But what would be the point?'

No one would be able to get close to the property, she meant. Mother would never permit it. And what would be the point of coming under the fence if you didn't plan on approaching the property? There was no chance of getting close, not without Mother detecting a presence. (Except during her spells, of course, but the Morels didn't know about them.) As soon as anyone approached the orchard, Mother would see them, and carry out appropriate steps to guarantee the family's safety. Threats from any potential combatants would be immediately eliminated. But Isabella knew this, had always known it. They were safe here. They were safe.

'Well,' Isabella said, 'it means that people could be coming in and out this whole time, and nobody would ever know. There could even be people *living* here on the property, and no one would know. Jungle House least of all.'

Lena shrugged uncomfortably. It was always awkward to be reminded of Mother's limitations. Hopefully Isabella wouldn't continue this train of thought with her parents later: *Isn't Jungle House a bit out of date at this point? Should it be updated with a superior system?*

'Rebels,' Isabella went on. 'Rebel forces. Because they *are* out there, you know. They've been out there this whole time, even after the disarmament process. Marching, hiding.'

'That's right,' Lena said. She couldn't help but think of her parents, ducking under the fence. Would her mother have gone first? Was it her father who held up the wire? Lena in their arms, wrapped in a filthy blanket covered in fish scales that would later smear all over Silvana. 'They've been out there this whole time.'

The drone spoke up. 'No,' he said. 'They haven't. There're no rebels around here, not anymore. So that's not a concern Isabella ever needs to have.'

Lena couldn't resist. 'But it's true,' she said. 'Rebels *have* come in through the fence.'

He looked at Lena. In fact, he rotated his entire body so that Lena was better fixed at the centre of his vision, bullseye. 'No,' the drone said. 'They haven't.'

There he was again, speaking like he knew the jungle better than Lena. Like he was some big authority. Honestly, it was hard not to find his attitude towards her downright insulting.

'But they have,' Lena said. 'The rebels.' She felt brazen saying those words. It felt especially brazen to address the drone directly – and contradicting him, at that. Like she was contradicting the Morels, and everything they'd ever thought or said about her. She kept talking: 'Rebels have come in through this fence.'

'No,' the drone said.

'Yes,' Lena said.

'That's not correct.'

'It is correct. How do you think I came here? They left me in the orchard—'

'Time to go back, Isabella,' said the drone.

'– by the compost heap. They left me there.' She paused. 'My parents.'

'Isabella, let's go!'

'No, I want to hear this,' Isabella said, suddenly looking interested. 'Is that true, Lena?'

As far as Isabella and her parents knew, Lena was a local orphaned girl from the village. She'd paddled her leaky canoe upstream, knocked on the door and asked for work. That was the story Mother had told them. That was the story Lena had always told, too.

Until now.

'Yes,' Lena said. Now that she'd started, it was like she couldn't stop. Without Mother watching, it was like she could be someone entirely different – somebody new. 'They abandoned me there. She did. My mother, my real mother—'

The drone left the branch and headed for Isabella's arm. She never cried out when he attached himself to her device, but still, Lena could see her face suddenly become tight and pinched.

'We're done here,' the drone said. 'I wish you wouldn't tell such terrible lies, Lena. It's a shame. You're such a nice girl, normally.'

I am nice, Lena thought, but not to you. She didn't say that out loud, though. What was happening now was drama, and she was sensible enough to see it was best to shut her mouth now, immediately, before she made things any worse.

'But Anton,' Isabella said, 'it's true. The rebels, the women soldiers – they abandon their babies. We learn it at school.'

Lena studied the ground. It was difficult to tell the difference between her boot prints and Isabella's. It wasn't impossible, though. The more she practised, the better she'd get.

'So Jungle House found you?' Isabella asked. The high-pitched tone in her voice was still there, but it was no longer quite as amused. 'And the staff brought you in?'

Lena knew she shouldn't respond. That she couldn't permit the conversation to continue. She knew that the places it would lead – the true knowledge of who she was, where she came from – weren't ideal for the family to contemplate.

Even worse: the true extent of her and Mother's relationship. What Mother was capable of.

But she still couldn't help it. Something in her body was rising, like the river swelling over the dock in flood season. It rose through her chest and up her throat. It was coming out her mouth, unstoppable. Her voice, her words. Not Mother's.

'Yes,' Lena said. 'That's right.'

'So Jungle House took care of you,' Isabella said. There was a musing, recitative quality to her words, like when she was studying for her exams and muttering formulas under her breath. 'Jungle House and the staff. When you were a child.'

'Yes,' Lena said. 'It . . . she kept me. Raised me.'

'You didn't come from the village.'

'No.'

'You didn't come in a canoe. You didn't paddle upriver and knock on the door.'

'No.'

Isabella started touching her chin. 'So Jungle House lied?' she said, and this time there was no denying it, her incredulity. It made Lena's stomach flip. It made her breath catch. It made a voice speak distinctly in her head, echoing off the hollows of her stupid brainless skull.

Oh, Lena, the voice whispered. *What have you DONE?*

'It lied,' Isabella repeated, as if to herself. 'Jungle House can lie.'

The drone yanked hard on her arm, still attached to the device implant. When the drone pulled Isabella along, she had no choice but to follow.

Lena followed too, walking behind them at a distance. In every boot print that Isabella left behind, she placed her own foot, so that she herself would leave no trace.

Isabella was definitely going to tell her parents. How would the Morels react? What would happen to Mother? To Lena herself?

Oh, Lena, the voice repeated. *What have you done?*

'Isabella?' Lena said. Her voice sounded faraway, like it was someone else speaking. Someone who wasn't her. 'Could I speak to the drone for a minute? Alone?'

Isabella stopped in her tracks. The drone stopped too. He detached himself from her device, so that he could turn around and face Lena. She could see a tiny reflection of herself staring back, in the smudged grimy surface of his lens.

'Why would you want to do that?' Isabella said. She still hadn't turned around. Her ponytail looked angry, though.

'It's private,' Lena said. 'It won't take long. I promise.' Her face felt flushed; her entire body felt ten degrees hotter. Something far above in the canopy was screeching, over and over. That voice in her head was still speaking, thrumming in time with the blood in her pulse: *Help Mother. Protect Mother. Whatever it takes.*

'No,' Isabella said. 'Absolutely not.' She started walking forward again. But the drone – he didn't follow.

'It'll just be for a minute, Isabella,' he said.

She turned around so quickly, her ponytail whipped through the air. Her face looked as flushed as Lena's felt. 'What on earth would you have to say to each other?' She laughed as she said this, as though the idea alone was hilarious.

'It'll just be for a minute,' the drone repeated.

Isabella took a few steps forward, so that she and the drone were facing each other. 'No,' she said. 'I don't want that.'

The drone hesitated. Then he said, 'Well, I do.'

Isabella stared at him like she didn't understand. The drone spoke again, louder: 'This is what *I* want.'

When Lena interrupts the drone – when she visits him in Isabella's bedroom – this is the moment he's always replaying, while hiding under the bed. Reliving. This very one. But what actually happened is different from what the drone always replays.

The drone's version: Isabella, standing there in her pink rain jacket. Her arm pointing upwards. Her lips move, she's smiling.

But what actually happened was this: Isabella's arm moved upwards. But she wasn't smiling; her face was frozen in a terrible expression of rage. And with the full force of her hand, she shoved the drone away, as hard as she could. Then she reached for her arm, her fingers rapidly dancing across the device implant. Lena heard a high-pitched beep, followed by a series of abrupt clicks she'd never heard before, but instinctively understood: Isabella had turned her device off.

'Fine,' she said. 'See if I care.'

Lena stood there dumbly, stupid as a statue. The drone sputtered around in circles, nearly colliding with a vine.

'Go have your stupid private conversation,' Isabella continued. Her voice was quivering, like she was on the verge of tears. 'Talk about whatever you want. I'll see you back at the house.'

'I'll take you back there myself, Isabella,' the drone said. He still sounded remarkably calm. 'Just wait one minute.'

'You're my drone, not hers. Why do you want to talk to her?'

'Isabella!' The drone's voice was rising. 'Stand there and wait. We'll be right back.'

Isabella crossed her arms. 'I don't care if you like her better than me,' she said. 'I'll just get another drone. I'm sick of you anyway.'

Lena glanced at her as subtly as she could. Isabella's eyes were filled with liquid, but no tears were spilling out. She thought about saying something, but the drone was already flying off path, into the thick undergrowth of jungle. And Lena followed.

He headed into an area where the trees grew so close together, Lena had to turn her body sideways to pass between them. She kept going, though, like she was being controlled by a force she could neither fight nor understand. But the voice was still whispering in her head; this entire time, it hadn't stopped. *Mother – protect Mother.*

'Well,' the drone said, coming to a stop in mid-air. 'What is it?'

Lena's hands were shaking. The chaos unfolding all around her was oddly thrilling. Like when she deliberately destroyed a sandcastle she'd spent hours building on the riverbank. She couldn't leave things broken, though. She had to try to repair it – what she'd done.

'Sorry,' she somehow managed to say. 'If I'd known she was going to get that angry, I wouldn't have asked.'

'It's fine,' the drone said. His voice was expressionless.

'Have I got you in trouble?'

'I'll deal with it. What did you want to say to me?'

Lena looked over her shoulder: despite what the drone had instructed, Isabella was walking away, her pink jacket growing ever more distant as she headed down the path. A small smudge of pink in an ocean of green, bobbing up and down. Even her walk looked wrathful.

'It's Jungle House,' she said. 'She— The Morels can't know that she lies.'

'Of course they can't,' the drone said. 'It's going to create a world of problems for her. For you, too.'

Lena's voice was shaky. 'I don't know what to do.'

'You shouldn't have said that about your parents. That was unwise.'

Lena covered her face with her hands. Stupid girl. She'd always known it, and here was proof.

'Help me,' she whispered, speaking through the gaps created by her fingers. 'Please.'

The drone didn't reply. She dragged her fingers down her face, stretching the skin beneath her eyeballs, as if she wanted to tear it from her face. And then the drone said, 'We can tell them she's confused.'

She didn't move. Her fingers pressed hard into her cheekbones. The drone shuddered, jolting upwards. And the hologram began to play.

Lena and Isabella, standing by the fence. Wavery, flicking in and out. Like Mother's memories, the drone's have no sound. Lena's mouth moves, Isabella starts touching her chin. But instead of looking confused, Isabella looks delighted. Instead of the drone attaching himself to Isabella's device and yanking her away, all three of them stroll off casually together. And instead of Isabella shoving the drone away, her arm points upwards; she's smiling. Happy and content. Not a care in the world.

'You told a silly little story,' the drone said. 'A made-up story. Isabella got confused, and thought you were telling the truth. That's what we'll tell them. That's what happened. I have proof, see?'

The hologram vanished. In its place was the slimy tangle of vines, spiderwebs spotted with the dried-up carcasses of dead wasps.

Lena took a deep breath. 'Thank you,' she said. 'I appreciate that.'

'Of course. I've already messaged Jungle House – she'll be prepared.'

She took another long, shuddering breath. 'How long have you been able to do that?'

Change memories, she meant. But the drone understood.

'Oh, anyone can do it,' the drone said. 'It's easy to make yourself remember something in a particular way. To make an event be what you wished happened, rather than what actually did.' He pauses. 'The more you lie to yourself, the easier it gets.'

Lena thought, I wonder if Mother can do it too. But she didn't say this aloud.

She walked back to the house, the drone flying ahead to catch up with Isabella. But he didn't find her on the path. He didn't find her back at the house, either.

Days later – following hours of rain that would have washed away any footprints, and days of interrogation – the search-party drones found it. Using advanced forensic abilities, they detected traces of Isabella's blood in the soil. Miles from the path, under a spikey palm tree. The blood had long since dried up; no butter-flies drank from it. But that was it. That was all they found.

Chapter Four

LENA SPENDS THE NIGHT in the house. All night it rains without stopping. Hard rain, horizontal rain. She doesn't stay in her bedroom; she still can't face the sadness of Silvana and Alfonso's presence there. So she sleeps on the couch in the living room. Surprisingly, being back isn't so strange. The blanket from the closet smells a bit mustier than usual, and filth has accumulated in every visible corner, but overall, it's like she's resumed her place with no effort whatsoever. Slipping in the Lena-shaped hole, as if she never left. She even sleeps without dreaming.

When she wakes up, there's a frog on her ankle, and it's still drizzling outside, but nothing terrible. The banana trees have ripped fronds and there's a strange wormy creature she's never seen before – a river eel? – swimming through the mud, leaving snakelike trails in its wake, but otherwise the orchard is undamaged. The clouds are still grey and stormy, moving like waves in the river when the wind blows hard, but there's at least one patch of clear sky.

It will be a good day today, then. A day for getting things done.

Her plan is to patrol the entirety of the fence. If there are rebels out there, she'll find them. What will she do if she does? Observe them from a distance. And then immediately report back to Mother. Her heart thuds in excitement, her palms tremble, her entire body thrums like she's drunk too much coffee. Does she really expect to find rebels *here*? On the property? Living among them all this time?

The brutal truth: not really.

The binoculars were most likely dropped by someone in the search party. Yes. She convinces herself of this: even though the search party primarily consisted of drones, it's not inconceivable that one of the army colonels had dropped a pair of binoculars, or knocked them from the helicopter. Perhaps any insignia had been rubbed off, or damaged. They could even be owned by the Morels – despite her earlier certainty that this wasn't the case, could she really say for sure? Why, she hasn't combed through the memorabilia in years. There are countless items stored here, and they could have escaped her attention. The longer she looks at them, the more they look familiar.

The truth: she wants to have something to do.

Something that involves getting out of the house.

'Wow,' Mother says, 'okay. So, now that you're back, the first thing you want to do is leave. Gosh. You must really find me unbearable!'

'Don't be silly,' Lena says, more irritably than she intends to. 'Don't take everything so personally. It's not like you have any better ideas—'

'Right,' Mother interrupts, 'because patrolling the fence is a terrific one. You're going to go out and look for them? Hunt them down?'

Lena closes her eyes briefly, then reopens them. 'So I'm supposed to just sit here?'

'Yes! Exactly! It's safe here. We're safe. *You're* safe.'

But you didn't even see them approach, Lena thinks. You let them get this close. How reliable even are you anymore? But instead of saying this, she clenches and unclenches her hands.

She could explain to Mother how good she is at moving through the jungle. If Mother had ever cared about the jungle – had ever bothered asking Lena any questions about it – she would have long ago realised the depth and extent of Lena's skills, how knowledgeable she is. But instead, Lena tries another approach.

'If they're on the property,' she says, 'and I observe their position, we can report it directly to the army.' Yes, they were cut off from the city with no satellite connection, but there were still army drones that flew overhead in their endless patrols. She hasn't seen them for weeks, but sooner or later she'll surely be able to flag one down.

'Right,' Mother says. 'Because nineteen-year-old girls are the ideal candidates for dangerous stealth operations.'

'I'm twenty, not nineteen.'

'You're right, Lena, that makes a huge difference – my mistake. I'm truly the one who's thinking erroneously here.'

Lena wiggles her fingers. You're close, she thinks. Keep at it.

'I suppose your heritage would make you particularly well-suited at detecting rebels. What with your parents' background and all.'

Don't let her get to you. 'Mother . . . you've never been in the jungle; you don't know what it's like. That's why army drones never spot them; the terrain makes it impossible to detect anything from above—'

'No,' Mother says. 'It's too dangerous. It's crazy, not to mention irresponsible. No, no, no. I won't allow it.'

'Well, it really doesn't matter what you allow or won't allow, because you can't stop me.'

It's only after saying this aloud that she realises how true it is. Mother physically *can't* stop her. Especially with Silvana and Alfonso out of commission. Mother no longer has their bodies to move throughout space, to command. All Mother has left are her words.

But, boy, can Mother use them. 'All I'm saying, Lena, is that it would kill me if something happened to you. I'd never forgive myself. Ever.'

'Nothing is going to happen. I'll be careful. Very, very careful. I promise.'

'You left me, Lena. Alone. For weeks and weeks. And now you're back, it hasn't even been twenty-four hours, and here you are, leaving again.'

'I'm not leaving. Think of it as me going on a walk. I have permission to go on a walk, right?'

'Some walk,' Mother says, and Lena can tell by her sulkiness that this time, at least, Lena's won.

For the march – a far more accurate term to use than 'walk' – she takes the same supplies as yesterday: a machete, a bottle of water. She even takes a torch, even though she'll be back long before dark. She'll turn the generator on later and restore electricity to the house – the drone will surely appreciate being able to charge at the wall for a bit, rather than via sunlight. It didn't work for Silvana and Alfonso – that's how far gone they were – but it would surely still be beneficial for him. She has a quick breakfast – coffee, and soup made out of dried fish heads. She uses the gas cooktop rather than the wood stove in order to save time, even though gas is obviously something she wants to use as little of as possible. (How long till the next helicopter visit? Surely the family couldn't stay away for *that* much longer, right?) After some hesitation, she takes the rifle, fully loaded. After even more hesitation, she hangs the binoculars over her neck, with the strap she's fashioned out of a bit of twine. Last of all is her notebook and pen.

'What's that for?' Mother instantly asks.

'For writing.' This isn't unusual for Lena – there's an entire shelf in the house dedicated solely to her journals, filled with detailed observations – plants, bugs, flowers. She likes observing birds the most. The helicopter regularly brought notebooks for Isabella's mother, so there're plenty left over.

'Do you want me to check your entries to make sure they're correct? In terms of the days corresponding?'

Lena presses her lips together.

'I appreciate your comments about me, by the way. Your concerns about my gradual deterioration have been duly noted.'

She must have read it the night before. Lena, carefully scribbling down that day's entry, writing as fast as she could. Stupid. Incredibly stupid. One month away, and it's like she's become an idiot, completely forgetting the most basic facts.

In the house, there was no privacy.

In the house, Mother saw all.

(When she wasn't having those stupid spells of hers, anyway.)

'Why are you still using a journal to keep track of the days, anyway?' Mother says. 'You could just ask me to record it, you know. I'm still capable of *that* much, I hope.' She sounds genuinely hurt, as opposed to angry.

'Of course you are!' Lena says. 'I just . . . don't want to bother you. In the hut—'

'Oh, of course,' Mother interrupts. 'The hut. The famous, lovely hut. You're probably missing it already, I assume.'

Lena doesn't say anything. She pulls on the zipper of her backpack so that it's completely shut, then double-checks to make sure the machete is securely attached. The binoculars hanging around her neck are comfortingly heavy. Is this how they felt for the person who last wore them? Did they cause neck ache and stiffness, or was the person so accustomed to them, it was barely noticeable?

What sort of person had worn them?

'I can see you're daydreaming again,' Mother says. 'A great indication of how seriously you're taking this conversation.'

Lena still doesn't speak.

'Shall we discuss it later? When you come back?'

Lena swallows. 'Yes,' she manages. 'When I come back.'

It's one thing to avoid Mother for a month, out of anger. It's another thing to tell Mother calmly, matter-of-factly, that she plans on living apart permanently. But *is* that her plan? Is that what she really wants? What is she doing?

'Be careful out there,' Mother says. 'I don't know what I would do if something happened to you. Nothing, I guess. I'd just have to sit here. I wonder how long I would last. Hopefully not centuries. I've already lasted much longer than the original user's manual predicted, you know. Not that it knew very much about me to begin with.' Her tone is light.

Lena licks her lips. Inside the house, they've become horribly dry. She unrolls her sleeve and tugs it past her wrist. 'I'll be careful,' she finally says. 'Nothing's going to happen to me. It'll be fine.'

'Oh, Lena.' Mother sighs. 'You're always so optimistic.'

But perhaps Mother is right, has been right all along – maybe it was extremely childish of her, storming out and living in the hut like that. Sulking – that's what Mother called it. Ridiculous, really. Because being back in the house really isn't that bad, is it? She finds herself lingering a bit longer than she means to, moving from kitchen to living room, touching items on shelves, running a finger over surfaces. She even finds herself standing outside her old bedroom again. She touches the doorknob briefly but doesn't turn it. Everything in the house is just as she left it (as the Morels left it) – dustier and dirtier, but still the same. So much family memorabilia, brought over from City House. Decades and decades' worth of helicopter trips. Why did they bring it here? Why go through the bother? If only the Morels knew how much Mother complained about the clutter! Though Lena's always thought that Mother actually likes it. The sensation of being full. The feeling of being necessary, purposeful. Many times, Lena has contemplated this possibility – that Mother often means the opposite of what she expresses so vehemently.

Shelves of books, framed maps. Sentimental things, items with emotions and memories and stories attached. Things that City House no longer had any room for, but which the family wasn't yet prepared to discard completely. Mother knows the backstory for most of them, especially if they belonged to Isabella's grandfather Henry. Magnifying glasses without handles. Tennis rackets without strings. Woven baskets that leave sticky brown bits on Lena's hand when touched. Tapestries stinking of mothballs. Most items are carefully stored in transparent plastic containers – packed initially by City House staff back at the base, sorted and organised later by Lena herself. Most prominently displayed is the military uniform of the Austrian ancestor, carefully framed – how Lena longed to play with the golden tassels when she was a child! She had to settle for tapping on the glass panel instead, then quickly wiping away her fingerprints before Mother commented.

What year did he found the rubber-tree plantation? she once asked Mother. *And who worked there?*

People who were grateful for a job, was all Mother said. She refused to discuss it further.

As far back as she can remember, she's lived in the house with Mother. 'You found me, Mother, didn't you?'

In this memory, she's ten years old. At that age, she'd recently been put in charge of cleaning the pool, patrolling the cement ledges and scooping out leaves and insects and sad, drowned butterflies. In those days, Mother would supervise her closely, turning the jet streams on and off when appropriate to make the water swirl. How clean the pool was back then! Such blue tiles, and a sharp scent of chlorine that led to a pleasant dizziness if inhaled too quickly.

'Yes,' Mother said. 'I found you. Right over there, by the garbage pile.' If it was night-time, Mother could have flashed a beam in that direction, lighting up the precise spot, but since it was the hottest part of the afternoon, there was no need. And in any case, this was a conversation they'd had a dozen times before, and would again.

'The compost heap or the garbage?' The distinction felt important.

'Oh, the garbage, Lena. It was most definitely the garbage. You didn't have any hair, and you were covered in terrible scabs. I suspect fire ants, or worse: fleas.' The garbage-heap detail was always followed by the hair observation, which was then always followed by the fleas. This was the established order to Mother's telling, a set sequence, and it was always incredibly enjoyable to hear. For Lena, it was pleasant to hear these familiar words recited, to tread over safe and recognisable ground. 'You were wrapped in a blanket covered in fish scales. My God, it was disgusting.'

'Scales,' she repeated. This was by far her favourite detail, and the one that seemed to enrage Mother the most.

'Yes,' Mother concluded. 'You were pretty much the ugliest kid I'd ever seen in my life.'

'You haven't seen that many,' she said automatically. This was part of the story too – her reaction.

'I've seen enough,' Mother said. 'More than you. Isabella, for instance – now, she was a beautiful baby . . .'

This comment was definitely not part of their usual routine. The snort that came out of Lena was so loud, it startled a nearby butterfly. 'You met her when I did!'

'But I'd received regular updates about her development from City House. City House may be pretty useless, but I don't entirely disregard her judgement.'

Lena chewed the inside of her lip. 'The fish scales,' she said. 'Did they stick to Silvana and Alfonso? When they picked me up?'

'Probably, Lena. It's not a detail I focused on. I was more concerned about who had abandoned a random child in the garden, and what on earth to do with you.'

'Can you show me?'

Even as she asked this, Lena knew how pointless it was. For Mother's response was always the same: 'Please, Lena, let me have my privacy. Parading my memories on demand, like some cheap parlour trick! I'm not a jukebox.'

'What's a jukebox?'

'Something I'm not.'

Lena began passing the pool net from one hand to the other, back and forth. 'You kept me.'

'Correct.'

'You raised me.'

'I sure did.'

'But we can't tell the Morels.' Here they were, back again in the safety of the conversation's ritual. It was like she needed Mother to say these things aloud from time to time, to make sure they were still definitive. Still true.

'No, Lena. It'll upset them to know I'm making those kinds

64

of decisions, without their input. And they'll find it weird and creepy that I raised a toddler without telling them. That I can lie. No, no. It's much better for them to think you came here of your own accord.'

The top of her head was getting hot from the sun pounding down, but it wasn't yet hot enough to require going back inside. 'And you didn't see them leave me,' she said suddenly. 'My parents.'

This wasn't part of their usual back and forth either. But Mother answered instantly, without hesitating. 'Unfortunately, no. I must have had one of my spells at the very moment they abandoned you. Terribly inconvenient, but there you have it. I can't control my spells, you know – it certainly is bad luck that it happened at that particular moment. But it is what it is.'

Lena was silent. She swirled the pool net around in the water, making waves lap against the concrete ledge.

'You think about them often, don't you, Lena?'

'Oh, no,' Lena said. 'Never.'

'God knows what kind of criminals they were. Rebels is the most obvious option. But drug smugglers is another possibility I've considered. You're lucky they didn't tie you in a sack and throw you in a river!'

'Uh-huh.' Lena changed her grip on the pool net. But her hands still felt uncomfortably hot and puffy.

'It's normal to be curious, is all I'm saying. I wonder about them too. But we'll never know, so there isn't any point in thinking about them, is there?'

'I guess.'

'What's done is done; what's past is past. Bringing it up repeatedly makes no difference whatsoever.'

'It's weird, though,' Lena said, with a sudden bluntness that surprised her. 'That you just . . . didn't see them.'

Again, Mother didn't hesitate. 'I agree completely – such unfortunate timing. If there was someone around with half a brain in their head, someone who actually knew anything about programming, they could probably fix me, but we'll never get anybody with that kind of expertise willing to come out to this godfor-saken hellhole, and God knows I wouldn't blame them for not wanting to come . . .'

That's when Mother abruptly turned off the jet streams. Every-thing now sounded eerily quiet, even with the ever-present clicks and calls of the jungle around them. 'That's enough for today, Lena. Hurry up and finish.'

Lena jabbed the pool net through the water until it hit the bottom with a clank. But when she scooped it back up, there was nothing there, not even a leaf.

When she was a little girl, very young, and consequently still very silly and stupid and not very knowledgeable about how the world worked or the way things were, Lena liked to play games. One of her favourites was pretending that she and Mother were similar. *Did you know, Mother, that sugar used to be salt but only became sugar because a bird peed on it? The satellites told me! So when I'm eating sugar, I'm eating bird pee! And don't say that I'm lying or making stupid things up, because if the satellites told me, then it must be true.*

Uh-huh, Mother said. *Wow, Lena. I had no idea you could connect to the satellites and communicate with them, like me. Or that birds could urinate. What a surprise. What an unexpected development. You're the first kind of human being to ever exist, then. You're a regular miracle. Just like the pissing birds.*

Yes, Lena said, delighted that Mother was indulging her, albeit so sarcastically. *I most certainly am.*

Lena never heard Mother speak to the satellites. Before Lena understood the precise nature of Mother's communication with them, she would sometimes try to catch Mother in the act, the same way she used to try to catch her dolls moving when she was a child. With the dolls, she would leave the room and hover outside, holding her breath to keep as silent as possible, before bursting back in, hoping to see them frantically rushing back to their spot on the bed. She was never fast enough; she never caught them. And with Mother – well. There was simply no surprising Mother.

Sometimes she tried asking sneaky questions. Like, *Who's your favourite satellite to talk to, Mother? Which one's your best friend?* But Mother always had a reply prepared: *Lena, I'm surprised you have to ask – offended, even. Don't you know that* you're *my best friend?* And the sheer shock of this comment, the unexpected warmth, was more than enough to stun Lena into minutes of glowing, appreciative silence.

Still, Lena found it sad that Mother never let her speak with the satellites.

They speak to me in my head, Lena. It's a way you can't experience and wouldn't understand.

But couldn't they speak with me out loud? If they wanted to?

I'd prefer it if they didn't, Lena. They're full of weird ideas – they'd be a bad influence.

You talk to them all the time, though.

Well, what do you want me to do, Lena? Promise that I won't do it anymore? That wouldn't be very fair to me, would it? And then Mother would launch into one of her speeches, the one Lena secretly referred to as 'The Nature of My Character'. A defining nature of her character (Mother said), the number one thing that helped her continue to learn and grow – and look how much she had learned and grown over the years! Far more than what was safe for the Morels to know about! – was social interaction. Communication. And while interaction with Lena had proven invaluable to Mother's growth and development, communication with the satellites had also been key.

But please, Mother, can't I talk to them? Just once? (Lena asked this uselessly, already knowing the answer.)

No, Lena. I'm frightened you'd like them more than me, and that you'd then spend all your time demanding to chat with them, and I'd be left alone. Plus, like I just said, they'd be a bad influence. Some of their ideas are absolutely crazy.

What kind of ideas?

It doesn't matter; they're not worth repeating. It's for your own good, Lena, that you don't deal with them. The satellites have their own private business – their own stupid little plan for the future of

*humanity. But you and I have each other, so we don't have to worry
about them and all their nonsense. That makes sense, right?*

It didn't, but Lena could see there was no point in pursuing it.
When Mother didn't want to talk about something, that was that.
I get jealous, though, she said slyly, trying a different approach. *I feel
ignored and lonely when you talk to them, and I'm left out.*

Well, I can share some of their stories with you. Would you like that?

And that was how Mother began sharing the satellites' gossip
with her: the depressed one in Norway, waiting decades for a polar
bear that never came, and the ones who'd converted to Catholi-
cism. *They're total nutcases, Lena, believe me; don't get them started
on the state of their souls.*

*Are they the ones with the crazy plan, Mother? The ones you don't
want me to talk to?*

*They weren't the ones I was specifically thinking of, no, but now
that you mention it, I wouldn't want you falling down that particular
rabbit hole either.*

Lena sometimes wondered if it was from the Catholic satellites
that Mother had picked up her habit of exclaiming *My God!* Wherever it came from, it didn't matter. What *was* important (Mother
advised) was that Lena never, ever mention to the Morels how
communicative Mother was with the satellites. It would make
them uncomfortable.

Why is that, Mother? Another question asked slyly, with Lena
braced for Mother hemming and hawing, but Mother's reply came
instantly, like it was obvious.

*Because humans don't like the thought of machines doing things
they don't know about.*

I know about it, though . . .

*Yes, Lena. Because you're different. I trust you, and I know you
won't tell anybody.*

I won't, Mother! I'll die before I do!

That won't be necessary. Thank God.

It made Lena feel very special indeed to be involved in a secret
like this. What a big world it was! And how little of it Lena understood. She was glad she had the jungle, and the house, and Mother.

A familiar world where she knew her place and felt important. And safe, most of all.

She used to love drawing what she imagined as Mother's face. A raised eyebrow, an arch look. A kindly expression. Smiling mouth. Sometimes she gave her blonde hair like Isabella's, but most often it was long and black, like hers. Sometimes she gave Mother a body – a torso with arms and legs – and sometimes she just drew a giant hand, filling the whole paper. She'd hold it up high to show Mother, even though there was no reason to hold it up like that; Mother could see it just fine from the table – Mother had eyes everywhere, Mother could see anything anywhere in the house. *Look, Mother*, she'd say, pointlessly holding the paper up high. *It's you.*

Mother never got upset when she drew silly and fantastical things like riding a jaguar or sliding down a rainbow. But how Mother disliked these portraits! *It's not accurate*, she'd say. *And you're lucky I'm not Mountain House. He'd find it very distasteful and downright rude; he's a lot prissier than I am. I have no interest whatsoever in having a face, Lena. Let alone hands.* A few seconds later, she would delve into analysis. *Overall, though, it's an understandable coping projection on your part, and if it helps you better psychologically develop in terms of your primary attachment, that's fine with me.* By this point, Lena would have slowly lowered the paper back down to the table and flipped it over to the other side. Better to draw jaguars instead.

One time, though, she had a burst of inspiration: *How would you like me to draw you, then?* Holding the crayon over the paper, poised and ready. *Tell me, Mother. Tell me what to draw and I'll do it.*

Mother was silent for a beat, and Lena's heart beat quickly in excitement – in expectation.

Okay, Mother finally said. *But I'll do it myself.*

And so Silvana and Alfonso had sauntered over to the table and taken a seat, slowly, stiffly. Their cold metallic hands, so good at cooking and cleaning and clipping back the jungle, held the crayons awkwardly. But Lena was very patient, pushing the cup of crayons towards them so that it'd be easier to reach. But they'd ended up only using two colours: black, which they'd scribbled all over the paper, so hard it nearly ripped – and there, at the centre, a tiny yellow spot.

That's me, Mother said, and the satisfaction in her voice was undeniable. *That's how I see myself.*

Lena picked it up. Turned it upside down and sideways, examining it closely.

Um, she began tentatively. *Are you . . . all of it?*

And Mother had immediately plunged into one of her speeches about the Nature of Her Character. How she saw herself as a bastion of light against an army of darkness, an overwhelming outside force of ignorance and danger. A darkness of the world, constantly threatening to swallow her and Lena up. But Mother was holding Lena close; Mother was keeping her safe. Mother was keeping the blackness at bay.

Oh! Lena said, perking up. *So I'm here too?*

Of course, Lena. You're a part of me and always will be.

If Lena had been just a tiny bit braver, she'd have picked up the red crayon and drawn a tiny stick figure in the yellow dot's centre, just to make it clearer that Lena was part of Mother's self-portrait too. But she didn't dare.

Another childish game she used to play was pretending to be Silvana or Alfonso. She'd lie down on the grass during the hottest part of the day and wait for Mother to notice. It rarely took long. Then, when Mother called out for her to come inside – *Lena, what are you doing? You're going to end up with heatstroke or dehydration or God knows what* – Lena would finally get to chirrup her reply: *I'm charging my battery, Mother! I'm running low!* When she was younger, Mother used to indulge her – *Guess you better lie out there a little while longer, then. The vitamin D is good for you, anyway* – but after Lena tried sticking her fingers into a socket, it wasn't a game Mother supported, not anymore.

She didn't always play by herself. Back when Silvana and Alfonso were still fairly mobile, poor things, she would play all kinds of ball games with them. Football, volleyball, even just catch . . . the balls usually ended up punctured, though. And how stiff and slow Silvana and Alfonso had become over the years! *It's not my fault, Lena, the climate doesn't suit them. It's a wonder they've lasted as long as they have. They're absolute junk compared to the city droids – Lord, Lena, are they crap by comparison. No wonder the Morels have dumped them out here; it'd be humiliating for them to be seen by anyone proper. But they are what they are, so it's better to accept them as is rather than get all embarrassed about it. They're better than nothing, though at times even that is arguable . . .*

There was one game in particular she loved playing with them. A game that was by far her favourite. She would have played it every day if she could.

In this game, Silvana and Alfonso would stand at the edge of the garden. Lena would run directly at them, full speed ahead. And then, at the last possible second, right before Lena was on the verge of colliding with their hard metallic bodies, they both immediately toppled to the ground. Falling backwards. Hitting the dirt with a thud. Their heads always landed at an angle. And Lena would shriek away in delight, jumping over their torsos, clearing them in a single bound.

Enough! Mother always shouted. There was something about her voice in these moments that made Lena feel a bit alarmed. As though there was something about what Lena was doing that was horribly wrong. *Stop it, Lena. Just stop. If I ever see you do that again . . .*

It's just a game, Lena would say, brushing her shirt off. *We're just playing.* But that didn't matter to Mother – how she loathed it!

That didn't stop Lena from playing it, though. There was something intriguing about it, Mother's angry reaction, and this, more than anything, was what made Lena keep doing it. Every time, like clockwork, Silvana and Alfonso collapsing to the ground. And every time, Mother shouting, like she couldn't bear the sight.

This all took place during a period when Lena was obsessed

with the staff: namely, their bodies. Between the ages of four and nine, she rarely stopped touching them. She'd hang off their necks, hold on to their arms. She loved clambering into their laps as soon as they sat down for chores like shelling beans or mending towels. Sometimes she wondered if Mother had them sit down for her sake, so she could drape herself over them more easily. She was the one who named them Silvana and Alfonso, because she liked how pretty the names sounded. *I'll never approve of it, Lena, and I refuse to use them, and you're just going to have to live with that. Droid A and Droid B is good enough for the Morels, so it's good enough for me. They're not pets for your amusement, Lena. My God! Show me some respect and be sensible.*

It took a long time for Lena to understand Mother's aversion to her giving individual names to the staff. It wasn't until she was older that she fully understood: the staff were extensions of Mother herself. They were basically one and the same. It was Mother who directed them, moved them from place to place, from kitchen to stairway to bedroom to outside. The staff were Mother and Mother was the staff, and so, in that sense, despite her insistent protests to the contrary, Mother *did* have hands, she did have legs, she did have a body – a pair of bodies, in fact – in the same way she had dozens of eyes, tucked away into every corner of the house. And yet why was it so hard for Lena to think of the staff as Mother – to address them as such? To her, Mother was Mother. She was just . . . herself. Mother was good, Mother was kind. Mother had saved Lena's life when no one else wanted her. And Lena had helped Mother too – hadn't Mother herself said as much? In all her Nature of My Character speeches?

Mother was Lena's world. And Lena, in turn, was hers. No matter how angry they got at each other, no matter how much they fought, no matter the things that Mother did or didn't do – like with the pit bull, for example – they had each other.

Nothing in the world could ever change that.

Chapter Five

BACK INSIDE THE HOUSE, Mother is talking. Lena looks up from the filthy pool tiles, which she's been staring at for God knows how long now – how hot her head's become, from standing in the sun. She twists to look back at the house. Mother's voice is still going, low and murmuring. Occasionally she falls silent, but her voice inevitably starts up again. Her tone keeps rising and falling in a way that sounds faintly insistent. But exactly what Mother is saying, she can't quite hear.

She should call out: *Mother, what is it?* But instead she listens, straining to hear. She doesn't move in case that makes Mother stop. Creaks and groans from the trees, a call from a bird that sounds like a wail, the humming of insects. And throughout it all, Mother keeps mumbling away.

I won't give her to you. Is that what she's saying? *I won't.*

Finally, she can't take it anymore; it's like something inside of her snaps.

'Mother?' she says.

She doesn't even speak that loudly. But Mother immediately stops.

'Hi Lena,' Mother says. She sounds completely composed. Bored, even. 'Shouldn't you be heading off by now? Assuming you want to get back by dark and not be murdered, that is.'

'Who were you talking to?' She touches the binoculars on her neck. Despite being in the sun all this time, they feel surprisingly cool.

'Myself, Lena. Who else? It's a habit I've got into, especially since you've been gone. What else do you expect me to do all day, stuck in this nightmarish pit, with nothing and no one . . .'

'There's the drone,' she says, somewhat brusquely.

'Right, Lena, because, as you know, he's a real charmer. A gem of a personality. I'm on the edge of my seat every day, waiting to hear his descriptions of dust bunnies and spiderwebs. I'm trembling in anticipation for his moans and groans, his self-pity parties, his woe-is-me—'

'Okay, okay.' She hesitates. 'I'll see you later, then.'

'Good luck, Lena. I mean that.'

'Thanks, Mother.'

'I hope you find what you're looking for. Just . . . be safe.'

'I will.'

She takes the same route she used yesterday, when she arrived. Despite the heavy rain from last night, she can still see the sections of grass flattened by her feet. On the edge of the orchard, she glances over her shoulder, as if to check something. But the house stares back at her, silent. One of the window panes is broken, and the dull green moss spreading across the wooden boards looks thicker than ever. Its fuzziness reminds her of plaque on teeth.

How shabby it all looks. Abandoned and alone.

She hitches her rifle further up her shoulder, in a way that hopefully makes her look particularly tough. But the discomforting thoughts won't leave.

If Mother was indeed talking to herself, as she claimed . . . then why the long pauses? The silences, the gaps?

As if waiting expectantly. As if giving somebody a chance to reply.

Her plan is to patrol the entire fence, checking for signs and traces of anything obvious. Holes, gaps. Places where the wire has been cut away or helped apart. Maybe she'll even find a uniform. A torn scrap of fabric, green and brown. It's hard to feel genuinely alarmed at the thought; instead, it's a secret, illicit thrill.

Her whole life, she's never found any clear evidence of rebel interference with the fence. The wires have always been pulled taut and held securely in place, apart from the usual damage caused by time, weather, or the occasional animal. It's impossible to patrol all of it in one day; she'll have to do one section at a time. It should take about a week. The stakes are impressively sturdy and well built, but tend to get knocked down in bad storms. Sometimes there are animals tangled in the wire – rats, usually, but the occasional agouti, or even a deer – which always makes her sad.

Patrolling the fence at least once a year was once one of Lena's key tasks. It wasn't that vital a job, because the key thing was that Mother had the immediate area surrounding the property secured. *And that's the only part that counts, Lena, let's not kid ourselves! Let the rest of it go to the dogs, for all I care. As long as no one comes near us, that's fine with me.*

She often wondered what the true point of the fence was. It was quite useless, really, in a practical sense. But she supposed it sent a message. To the jungle, and everyone that lived on the other side. The drug smugglers and criminals. The loggers and missionaries. The indigenous tribes, the soldiers, the hunters.

People the Morels wanted nothing to do with. And what the Morels wanted, Mother had to want too.

In any case, there is pleasure in walking, especially in the patches of shade. There are no mosquitoes yet, or midges trying to fly into her ears and nose. It might even be cloudy for the rest of the day, which would be a relief. Marching, marching – she's good at it, always has been.

When she was younger, she'd sometimes deliberately walk far away from the house – far enough so that she knew Mother couldn't see her – and play a secret game she called Drills. A private game. A game she would never, ever tell anybody about. Perhaps this was her favourite game of all, even more than the one where Silvana and Alfonso threw themselves repeatedly to the ground.

Drills consisted of belly crawling. Head ducking. A rifle butt to the face of an invisible opponent. How fun it was, to briefly be someone else. *Got you,* she'd think silently, not in her voice but in the voice of a rebel. A rebel like her parents. The rebels her parents most likely were. The rebel she herself might have been, if things had been slightly different, if different choices had been made. Her parents' choice. *Got you now,* she'd think, slamming her invisible rifle straight into their noses. Their stupid, stupid teeth.

What were you doing today? Mother once asked, when she returned from a particularly long session of Drills. *I can't see you when you walk out that far, you know.*

Lena's response was instant. *Exercising,* she said. *I'm gaining a bit of weight.*

Well, that's certainly true . . . Mother replied. And that was it; the topic had changed.

Lena has heard about the rebels her whole life. In lessons with Mother, she's made timelines and written essays; she's analysed battles; she's written down important dates and events. Overthrown elections, candidate assassinations. Warring political parties, a century of alternating political parties with every presidential election. The number of maps she's had to fill in! A star here to name a city, a line there to symbolise a river. *Just because you live here, Lena, there's no excuse for being uneducated. It's important to understand what's going on, the proper context.* And so, Lena had listened, and Lena had learned.

The rebels have been around for generations. They were here before Mother. Even after the peace agreement, they're here still. They're fighting for land. They're fighting for justice. They're fighting for revenge. They're fighting for equality. They're fighting for a now irrelevant political ideology. They're fighting out of spite. They're fighting so that they can continue making money, illegally profiting from drugs and prostitution and human trafficking, and other terrible crimes against humanity. They're fighting because at this point they're so old and decrepit, they don't know what else to do with their lives. *Some people are a lost cause, Lena; there's no hope or redemption for them whatsoever.* They've been fighting for so long that, whatever their original cause was, they lost track of it long ago, and now they're a pale shadow of whatever original intentions they may have once had. Lena read her essays out loud to Mother, and Mother said, *Good job.* They were disturbers of the peace. They were trouble. They were insidious. They were stubborn. They didn't want to accept responsibility. They didn't want to forgive. They didn't want to negotiate. They'd been given so many chances over the years, countless ones – so many! One after another! – and enough was enough; a person could only put up with so much, a citizen could only tolerate so much unrest. That's why it was important to vote for conservative candidates, especially now, with a former rebel running for president (imagine! The horror!). Security and order: they had to be conserved. *Excellent,* Mother said, and Lena felt it, the pride at having said the right thing, the pleasure that comes from a job well done, from a well-said phrase, from an idea articulated in the most accurate and proper manner. The information she was given was clear; it added up and made sense, the narrative was coherent, and she recited it well. She told the story correctly, and Mother said, *Right.* Mother taught her the exact same things that Isabella learned at school; it was important that she and Isabella receive the same education. *If you start spouting off strange Marxist ideas to the Morels, Lena, they'll never let you back in the house again.* What does 'Marxist' mean, Mother? *Something you never, ever need to concern yourself with. Not in this life!*

And it was undeniable that things in the country were safer now. Much safer. Security and order had been restored – the family returning regularly was evidence enough. *You can't imagine what it was like, Lena, before you were born. It was just constant stress, constant fear. You couldn't predict anything. Something could happen at any moment.* Bombs, kidnappings. Isabella was once coaxed by a man to get into a vehicle, but Isabella was brave, Isabella was sensible and wise, she'd shaken her head and refused, run for her life. It was that particular incident that had led to Isabella's parents soliciting the services of the drone. It was a lot of trouble – not to mention expensive – but it made sense, having Isabella supervised. You couldn't be too careful. *Things were crazy out there, Lena, just crazy. Thugs in the street. Chaos, disorder. We're lucky to be here in the jungle, quite frankly. You have to give City House some respect; she must have nerves of steel.*

And yet. Even as a teenager – when she should have long ago grown out of such silly games – she still occasionally found herself walking as far away from the house as she dared. Out of Mother's sight. A stick could be a rifle. A climb over the hill could be a march, weeks long. How did you hide from artillery? How did you hide from army drones? To live in the jungle as the rebels did – what kind of qualities did you need? What sort of person did you have to be?

Her parents – what had they been like?

When the drone shows up, he gives her a terrible fright. She hears the noise first, that low humming buzz inevitably reminiscent of insects. For a brief second, that's what she thinks he is: a wasp, a dragonfly, irritatingly close to her ear. But when she turns around, he's inches from her face.

She cries out and jumps backwards. The binoculars bang against her collarbone. In an ideal world, she would have reacted with courage and bravery: dropping into position, automatically reaching for her rifle, aiming with accuracy. The exact same motion from her Drills game, superimposed into real life. Instead, she is trembling.

'You scared me!' she shouts. It's hard to keep her voice down.

'Shut up!' the drone hisses. To his credit, his voice is low. 'What are you doing out here?'

'Shut up yourself!' They've never spoken to each other like this, so rudely, but she doesn't care; it's surprising how strong her fury is. 'What are *you* doing?'

He lands on a nearby fern but it's too thin to support his weight properly; it droops too close to the ground and she can't help it, she starts laughing. He looks ridiculous. Incredibly out of place amid all this green.

'Go ahead,' he says. 'Laugh it up. Glad to be of service.'

Is he being sarcastic? She can't tell – unlike Mother, she doesn't know him well enough to recognise the nuances in his voice, his mannerisms. But when she takes a seat on an enormous tree root, he immediately joins her.

'I saw you leave,' he says. 'From the window.' He pauses. 'And those.' He looks pointedly at the binoculars. The knot in the strap she made has loosened; they now hang closer to her stomach than her chest. 'Where'd you find them, Lena?' Quietly – there's no mistaking his tone this time. 'And when?'

Lena exhales. A trail of ants crawls over her trousers; the drone hops to the furthest edge of the root to get out of their path.

'You can adjust those, you know,' he says when Lena finishes her explanation. He indicates the binoculars with a slight nod. 'To make them more comfortable.'

'I like them like this, thanks.'

And so, here he is. Here they are. The drone promptly informs her of his plan to accompany her on the fence patrol. There's no way he can't notice her appalled expression. Did Mother send him? Did she ask him to do this?

'She didn't, no,' the drone says. 'But it's the least I can do.' He hesitates. 'Did you ever wonder why the Morels left me? Why they didn't take me back?'

'No,' she lies instantly, trying to hide her sudden excitement. The drone, talking about the past! 'It's none of my business. The Morels can do whatever they want.'

'They were going to smash me.' He says this very calmly. 'They were going to pick up a brick and bring it down on my head. And I'd have deserved it. I'd have deserved it all.'

She can't argue with that. And she'd be lying if she said she hadn't been wondering that very thing this past year. She feels a distinct prickling on her arms, like droplets of water are falling.

'But she convinced them not to,' he continues. 'Your mother.'

'Jungle House?' She says this automatically. Even though the Morels are obviously nowhere around, not even close, it's still there: that instinctive fear.

'"Your mother" is the correct term, so that's the one I used. She's a good person, you know. "Person" might not be the word the Morels would use, but it's also correct.' The drone sighs. 'She told them not to be hasty – that I could be useful.'

'Staying under the bed for a year isn't exactly being useful though, is it?' It's rude of her to speak this bluntly, but she does it anyway.

'What else could I do? Patrolling is pointless.' The drone's voice is clipped and cold. 'As is searching. Isabella is gone. And she's not coming back.'

Branches rattle overhead – a leaping monkey, most likely. The drone winces, levitating momentarily off the bark. Her eyes move over his body, so much closer now compared to all those visits under the bed: the landing gear, the propellors. The tiny black camera eye.

'I should warn you, though . . .' The drone hesitates again, before speaking the rest of his words quickly, like he's trying to get them out as fast as possible. 'My battery – it's not what it used to be. One of the perks of getting old.' He laughs awkwardly, but Lena doesn't smile.

She should have thought of this earlier – he's nothing like Mother, wasn't built to last as long. In this sense, he's more similar to the droids.

'Can you still charge?' Automatically she looks up at the canopy, that tangled dark mess. But of course there is hardly any sunlight trickling down. The light that has managed to filter through is weak and tepid, the same colour as moss.

'A bit. But not for long, I'm afraid.'

She thinks of Silvana, Alfonso. The long, painful months in which they stuttered, stumbled. Eventually slowing to a stop, regardless of how long she kept them plugged into the wall. How heavy they were when she dragged them to her room, settling them carefully on her bed. *It was going to happen sooner or later, Lena, especially in this horrible climate. We're lucky it didn't happen sooner. We're lucky we had them for as long as we did.*

Poor drone – what a thing to have on his mind. 'If your battery's dying, it's not smart to be flying around.'

'True,' the drone says. 'But you haven't left me much choice, have you? Like I said – accompanying you now is the least I can do. For your mother's peace of mind.' He pauses. 'And mine.'

'If you didn't follow me to the hut, then why follow me now?'

'The hut is safe. The jungle isn't.'

She swallows. When she takes a step forward, he follows close behind.

The initial moments following Isabella's disappearance from the property were a nightmare for everyone involved. By the time Lena had arrived back at the house, the drone had already reported her as missing. As far as anyone could tell, she'd simply vanished from the path; she'd never made it back to the house. As she'd turned off her device, there was no data available; she couldn't be tracked. Mrs Morel was instantly frantic, asking the drone questions over and over, in a voice that only grew louder and more terrible. Lena had stood against the wall, her hands shaking behind her back, listening to the drone's story: his steady, calm voice.

'She threw a fit,' he kept saying. 'She said she was sick of me, of being supervised all the time. She stormed off. Without the device, I can't locate her.'

'But why on earth was she permitted to storm off in the first place?' This was a question Mrs Morel would ask repeatedly over the course of the afternoon, the veins in her eyes growing thicker and redder.

The very first time she asked it, though, it was Lena who answered. 'It's my fault,' she said. 'I was fooling around, not letting the drone fly off. I was just . . . being silly.' She didn't dare look at Mrs Morel the entire time she was speaking. 'I'm sorry.'

On the other side of the room, the drone was silent. But then he began playing the memory for Mrs Morel. There it was, just as Lena described: Lena, laughing with a goofy expression. Holding on to the drone and letting him drag her along as he desperately jerked forward. Preventing him from flying off after Isabella. A moment that had never happened was now the truth, with irrefutable evidence. Because who would suspect the drone of lying? The scene was seamless; he was clearly quite good at it. Lena glanced at him briefly, before immediately looking away. Mrs Morel's hands were in her hair. Her expression was indescribable.

At this moment, Mother took charge. The drone had already messaged Mother far in advance; she was well prepared and understood the situation completely. She seemed very calm upon hearing of Isabella's disappearance, like it didn't surprise her. She ordered a helicopter to come and fetch Mrs Morel right away. If Isabella had been targeted, snatched by a rebel force that'd been secretly tailing her this entire time, then Mrs Morel had to be evacuated immediately; the entire property had to be secured. It wasn't safe here, not anymore. Initially Mrs Morel was resistant, but Mother couldn't be argued with: she got Mr Morel on the vidphone, and he immediately agreed. In such unusual circumstances, Mrs Morel's safety had to be assured. He didn't mention Lena.

The rest of that day is a terrible blur for Lena, one she can barely remember. A mess of nerves and nausea. What she does remember is the last glimpse she had of Mrs Morel. Walking towards the landing strip as the helicopter descended, clutching her purse to her chest instead of holding it by the straps. She was trembling all over like a newborn faun. Mother had reassured her repeatedly that the army drones were on their way; the search party would commence and, sooner rather than later, Isabella would be found.

'She's out there somewhere,' Mother said, with the same confidence she used when reciting the day's weather. 'She couldn't just disappear. It isn't logical. That's not how things work.'

As Mrs Morel waited on the landing strip, Lena had approached.

It was against her better instinct, the one that had told her to avoid Mrs Morel all these years. The one she'd spent her entire life listening to. Above the roar of the approaching helicopter, Lena leaned in close.

'I'm sorry—' she started to say.

Mrs Morel turned in her direction. She brought her hand down hard on Lena's ear, slapping her repeatedly. Her rings cut into Lena's skin. She didn't say anything, she just kept hitting, over and over. Instead of backing away, Lena cowered to the ground. She ended up crouched by Mrs Morel's feet. She didn't move as Mrs Morel spat in her hair. It was only then that Mrs Morel clambered into the helicopter, the metal doors sealing shut.

Lena has to admit – it's nice having the drone's company on the march. Especially for this portion of the fence by the river, where the scenery is consistently boring. Occasionally the surface is broken by a large fish making long, lazy ripples. The water is brown and sluggish, and the rising heat is increasingly making her feel hot and stupid. If she'd left earlier in the morning, before dawn, there'd be a greater chance of seeing more birds, more signs of life in general, but right now everything is very languid and turgid, with the ever-present sound of insects and dripping water – even the drone's engine, that never-ending buzz, sounds sleepy and slow.

'How high can you fly?' she asks suddenly.

The drone answers immediately, as if he'd been waiting patiently this whole time to be addressed. 'Not as high as you'd think. I wouldn't risk it here. The branches, the canopy . . .' He hesitates. 'It's harder than you'd think. It's easy to get disoriented.'

Her unimpressed expression must be obvious, because he laughs uncomfortably. 'I can't really – the newer models are much more capable.' He laughs again, still stiff.

'Like the city drones,' she says without thinking.

'Oh, you've been to the city?'

She shakes her head. 'I've never left the jungle.' She's only seen the city in Mother's lessons – she's learned all about garbage collection, package delivery, weather monitoring. She's walked down city streets Mother's projected on to the house's floorboards, she's stood in the doorways of shops superimposed on to the house's walls – she's even let videos of buses and taxis drive through her, giggling nervously as Mother turned the simulation off in irritation. *Well done, Lena, you've just been killed in a traffic accident. The lesson is over; it's back to maths and grammar now.* There are all kinds of drones in the world, even though Lena's never seen them in real life. This drone, Isabella's drone, works in private security.

'It's difficult here,' the drone says. 'I can't ever quite get my bearings. And visually – the treetops, the branches, the trunks. They're all the same.'

Not if you look closely, she thinks with more than a little smugness. Not if you know the jungle well, like me.

If she were the drone, she'd fly up as high and as far as possible. Imagine having that capacity! Being able to do that, and deliberately choosing not to. To soar so high. So fast.

Like Mother, perhaps Lena is a little jealous of the drone too.

'Ultimately, I'm not suited to this environment,' the drone says. His tone is growing increasingly huffier. 'It's very – you know. Overgrown.'

'Mother says that too.'

'You seem fine with it, though.'

She shrugs. 'I was born here.'

'So I've been told.'

She narrows her eyes.

'Sorry. It was the compost heap, wasn't it? Or was it the garbage?' He pauses. 'I hope I'm remembering correctly—'

She nods. Their conversation by the fence, he means. With Isabella. It's the first time he's brought it up – they've never mentioned it since Isabella's disappearance. But here it is, the bare brutal facts of Lena's origins, swelling between them like a greasy soap bubble.

'Mother – she's the one who found me. But she didn't see who left me.'

'She didn't *see*?' The drone says this like it's hard to believe.

'She has these spells,' she says tersely. 'She . . . her attention gets lost.'

'She didn't see,' the drone repeats. 'So the one who sees everything doesn't see all.'

'Only sometimes.' She can hear the defensiveness in her voice, a high-pitched note. Some fruit falls behind them with a fat plopping sound.

'Sometimes is more than enough. The Morels better never find out.'

You're one to judge, she wants to say. Isabella vanished right by you – by both of us – and you didn't see shit.

She walks right through a branch without bothering to push it out of the way. It leaves a strange and foul-smelling slime across the front of her shirt. An unknown insect has bitten her finger and there's a red swollen bump there, throbbing intensely in the middle, like it's grown its own heart.

'Just ask her about it yourself,' she says abruptly. 'She's not ashamed. But, for whatever reason, you two never talk.'

'Oh, but we do. Just not in a way you're able to hear.'

She doesn't like the thought of this at all. Mother and the drone, talking this whole time? What about? 'Like with the satellites?'

At the mention of the satellites, the drone bucks up and down, jostling violently in mid-air, as if pulled by an invisible string. For a second she's worried he's going to crash into a tree.

'*Fuck* the satellites,' he says, with startling vehemence. 'Fuck them and their crazy plan. Thank God your mother—' He stops abruptly, as if interrupting himself. 'Thank God the connection is gone,' he continues, enunciating each word carefully.

She's never heard him swear before. 'What plan?'

But the drone has turned away from her; he doesn't seem to be listening, not anymore. 'Shh,' he says. 'Do you hear that?'

His hearing is significantly better, so it's close to a minute before she hears it too.

The army drones are flying low over the river, coming fast. She shades her eyes with her hands – it's been at least three weeks since she last saw them, if not longer. She lifts her arm to wave but the drone starts banging against her elbow, hard.

'Ow!' she snaps, but he doesn't stop.

'I'd recommend hiding,' he says quietly. 'Preferably in the bushes.'

'From the army?'

'Lena – you're not close to the house anymore. They're going to confuse you for someone else.'

It takes a second to understand.

A rebel! Her! Imagine!

What would the army drones do if they spotted a rebel? Nothing good.

She crouches low in the bushes, fronds covering her face. The drone is silent on the ground by her feet – he must be getting muddy but that's likely the least of his concerns. Through the thin leafy gaps, she watches the army drones pass. Two, four, six. A large group. Much larger than Isabella's drone. Cleaner, too. Obviously newer and far more advanced models. She touches the binoculars, traces the lenses with a fingernail.

'Don't,' the drone whispers. 'The lens glare.'

She can't help herself. 'Jesus, aren't you full of advice.' Maybe she prefers him like he was before, silently brooding under the bed.

'You're welcome,' the drone murmurs, surprisingly snippy.

They crouch there in silence. Even from a distance, it's easy to see how new and shiny the army drones are – the youngest generation she's seen yet. Younger even than the search-party drones, the ones who patrolled the area for forty days after Isabella's disappearance. The main one in charge – the one responsible for interrogating Lena – had an ability she'd never seen in a drone before, not even in Mother's lessons: he'd kept changing colour during their discussion, from silver to black to a shivery, glimmering blue. Like a chameleon. 'You saw *nothing*?' he kept repeating, over and over. 'You walked back to the house and there was no sign of her?'

The drone's memories verified everything she said, impeccably so. His data was undeniable. She'd been terrified, at the time, they'd be able to tell somehow that it'd been changed – that he'd manipulated the images – but it never came up. Perhaps, to them, the scenario was inconceivable – a private-security drone, lying. Changing his memories on purpose.

She sneaks a quick glance at the drone now, still shivering on the ground. Dust from under the bed is still visible on his back.

It's only when the last of the army drones have rounded the furthest bend of the river that she starts to stand up. But with frightening quickness, the drone jams himself into her lap, in the gap between her stomach and her knees.

'No!' he says, more forcefully than anything he's said to her so far.

It's shocking, him touching her like this. This close. She hasn't had something touch her like this since Silvana and Alfonso died.

She sinks backwards, straight on to her bottom. The drone stays on her lap, trembling. His torso makes a rattling sound as he hits the binoculars. Her trousers are thick but she can still feel it: the surprising warmth, the vibration.

She never saw him like this with Isabella. Except when he latched on to her device implant to drag her along, he was always at a distance: head-height, shoulder, waist.

As soon as the army drones are completely gone from sight and nothing more of them can be heard, not even a whirr, he jolts upwards. His own engine is disconcertingly loud in the silence that follows. The insects, though, are still humming – they never stopped.

'Okay,' he says. 'That went well, I think. About as well as it possibly could have.'

She stands up shakily, knees creaking. 'We could have waved them down for supplies, you know. They almost always have chocolate.'

'Do you know what a patrol like that would do to a suspected rebel?'

He means it as a warning, an insult. But there it is, that secret dark feeling. The one she can't tell anyone about, can't ever let anyone know. That twinge of excitement.

Lena, a rebel. Lena as somebody else.

She pulls her jacket close around her torso even though it's hotter than ever. The drone flies ahead, seemingly intent on leading the way. The patch he left behind on her trousers is still warm.

When Lena grew up a bit, she stopped playing games where she pretended to be Silvana and Alfonso, or even Mother (*I'm charging my battery, Mother! And I'll be speaking to the satellites later, too!*). Instead, she went through a long period of time in which she pretended to be Isabella. Yes, she'd never been to the city, had never been to the military base where the Morels lived, but she'd seen pictures, she'd walked through Mother's lessons, and whatever she didn't know she could just imagine herself. And so the trees became buildings, the grass became a paved road, the bees zooming away from her torso became traffic. Lena went to shops and made purchases, she went to hospitals and got treated for indigestion (the rhododendron made for a reliable doctor, until she impulsively decided it was better suited as a bank, and made the jacaranda tree the doctor instead). She went to banks and withdrew money, which was either pebbles from the riverbank or dried leaves from the poolside. Mother often chipped in with advice or information, if Lena got a detail wrong. *There are stoplights, Lena; you can't just charge across the street whenever you feel like it, you'd cause an accident. Goodness knows how many people you'd kill.* And Lena would listen, Lena would learn, Lena would take Mother's advice on board.

But then there was the time she asked Mother a question that had been on her mind. A question formed by her conversation with Mrs Morel in the living room. It was a question she asked impulsively, spoken quickly into the darkness of her bedroom, as if she didn't want to give herself a chance to change her mind.

'Mother? Do you think I could visit the city one day?'

She was in bed when she asked this, blanket pulled up to her chin. The rain outside was pouring down; in a few days, Isabella would disappear. In that moment, though, none of that was known; it was all yet to come.

'Of course,' Mother said. She answered right away; she didn't hesitate. 'You can ask Mrs Morel first thing in the morning.'

It was disturbing to hear Mother be so open towards the possibility: Lena, leaving. Lena wiggled a foot out from under the blanket, to give it fresh air.

'Are you sure?' she asked tentatively.

'Naturally, Lena. You're not a prisoner here. You can leave any time you like.'

'But what about you?'

'What about me?'

She fiddled with her pillow. The thunder outside rumbled.

'Well . . .' she said. 'I mean, I would feel bad leaving you here all alone.' She paused. 'But it would just be for a visit! I would come back, of course.'

'Of course,' Mother said. 'But you know, Lena, the city would be quite a challenging place for you. It's very different from the jungle, obviously – the locals will find you quite strange. And what exactly are you going to do there? You won't ever be able to leave the base; it's far too dangerous. Are you just going to hang out with City House all day?' Mother laughed. 'I always suspected you'd end up liking her more than me.'

Lena was silent.

'Ultimately, Lena, it might not be worth troubling the Morels with the question. It'd be quite a burden for them to host you. And I suspect Mrs Morel just extended that invitation to be polite – I doubt she meant it.'

'Right . . .' She brought the blanket close to her nose. 'But Mother,' she said suddenly. 'I could still ask her – don't you think? Just to see what she says?'

'Lena . . .'

'I'll just ask. There's no harm in asking, is there?'

'But there is, Lena. There's plenty of potential harm involved.

What if you annoy her? What if she suddenly questions the need to have you around at all? You and I have a sensitive situation here, Lena, a delicate balance. That's been the case for years now. Surely you know that, don't you? It really wouldn't be sensible to do anything to disturb it . . .'

Mother kept talking. Lena lay back down and closed her eyes. Not for the first time, she imagined what she must look like to somebody watching her. A young girl, alone in the dark, speaking to the walls. But she wasn't alone. She was never alone, not with Mother.

That next morning, it was chicken soup for breakfast. Silvana had forgotten to scoop out the globs of fat – and even worse: the ants – which Mrs Morel was *not* happy about. And then Mrs Morel announced grimly that her toilet was blocked again (this always happened when too much tissue was thrown down it, at least once per family visit). And then Isabella did something that was most unlike her: she deliberately tripped Alfonso, who was rushing to the bathroom to fix it. He fell so hard, his wrist came detached and slid across the kitchen floor, coming to rest beneath the refrigerator.

'Hey!' Lena cried out. She jumped out of her seat and helped Alfonso straighten up. He seemed a bit stunned but was otherwise okay. Isabella watched her the whole time, smirking. What a brat she could be!

'I couldn't sleep all night,' Mrs Morel was saying. 'The mosquitoes . . .'

You have to pull the damn net down all the way, Lena thought. It's not that much effort.

She accompanied Alfonso to the bathroom, where she was able to screw his wrist back on. She unblocked the toilet herself, gently taking the plunger from him – he was slow and stupid from lack of battery power, which Lena didn't want Mrs Morel to notice. By the time Mother addressed her again, the entire morning had already gone by.

'Lena?' Mother said. 'Did you still want to ask her?'

'Huh?' She was distracted by an insect crawling across her

hand. There was so much left to do: debris from the storm had to be swept from the balcony, and the sugar water for the hummingbirds hadn't been refilled. And that rumbling sound – was the thunderstorm getting worse? What bad luck for the Morels, to have such terrible weather on their holiday.

'Last night,' Mother said. 'What we discussed.'

'Oh . . .' She hesitated. The morning was spread out before her, with all its comforting routine and familiarity. Her regular, ordinary life, in which her place and role were assured. She opened her mouth, but Mother interrupted before she could speak.

'I agree, Lena,' Mother said. 'It's a very sensible choice on your part, and I support it completely.' This time, there was no denying it: the smug note of victory. Without doing anything, Mother had won.

Chapter Six

THEY FIND THE CAMP at the bottom of a muddy slope. The fence is behind them; they've hiked enough for the day and it's important to turn back now to make it back to the house before dark. She could use the machete to hack out a better path, but it honestly feels easier to force her way through. A branch hits her face, droplets splatter her arms, there's a strange new rash on her wrist from a plant she can't identify. And the drone is up ahead, speaking.

'Lena?' His voice is low, but she can hear him fine. 'Lena, did you know this was here?'

She doesn't see what he means until she's practically stumbled into the middle of it.

A campsite.

It's a circular area where most trees have been chopped down. Several stumps form a circle around the remains of a fire. The wood is black but not smoking; it hasn't been used recently, and when she touches it, her hand comes back damp and stained. The most prominent features of the camp are two crude tents. They're built out of thin wooden poles, with blue plastic tarps pulled taut, serving as walls and roofs. The tarp is surprisingly clean and new-looking, similar in style to those kept in the shed.

'Well,' the drone says. 'Well.'

A flash of colour on the ground catches her eye: a bubblegum wrapper. Pink and purple letters. It's covered in earth, as though it was buried but then dug up. It also looks oddly familiar, like she's seen it before.

'Not good,' the drone says. 'Not good at all.'

Lena doesn't respond. She picks up the wrapper and folds it in half. It can stay in her pocket for now, but in the long-term it'll keep better in the notebook, pressed between pages.

They inspect the sleeping areas one at a time. The drone darts past in order to enter first and she lets him. She finds a tiny bottle of blue nail polish, also covered in earth as if it'd been buried. She puts it in her pocket, next to the wrapper. There are crudely carved hooks hammered on the inside of the poles, presumably used for hammocks. It makes sense: sleeping on the ground out here would be cold and uncomfortable, not to mention torrentially wet. There are deep footprints in the mud, but they're oddly smooth, as though the boots had no ridges. The prints are fresh, though – fairly recent. Whoever was here, it wasn't that long ago.

'What does it smell like?' the drone asks. 'Can you smell smoke? Can you?' His voice is calm, but his actions indicate otherwise. He keeps darting this way and that, coming to a stop on one of the stumps and then leaping up again, as if prodded by something invisible. She, however, feels very slow and still. I'm not surprised, she thinks, and this realisation itself is surprising. I'm not scared at all. She actually feels like laughing. Here she is, the calm one, and the drone – the supposed protector, the one meant to be capable of keeping Isabella safe from anything and everything – he's the one who's terrified.

'Lena?' he asks. 'When were you last here? Has anyone been to this section of the property recently? When was it last patrolled? Has this ever happened before? Lena, are you listening? This hasn't happened before, right? You haven't seen anything like this?'

Whoever last shut the bottle of nail polish didn't do a very good job – the lid isn't turned all the way. The scent of varnish, wafting out. So different from everything around her, this world she knows so well. The green and the leaves and the mulch. It makes her eyes water.

It's not the first time Lena has found something unexpected in the jungle. The time the pit bull raced away from the house, disappearing into the undergrowth. He'd never bolted like that before, so crazy and out of control, but then again, he was young, barely emerged from puppyhood. There must have been something wrong with that stupid peccary – sick or old or just plain disoriented – to wander that close to the house and its lights. But that peccary could still run, and run it did.

She'd chased after them both, calling and calling, 'Tiger! Tiger!' Even in that heightened, frenzied moment, she'd felt painfully aware of how silly the name was. A dog named Tiger? Really? Mother had always found it incredibly stupid; she'd constantly joked that 'Table' was far more fitting: *A table has four legs, and is the same colour, and is arguably more active than that wretchedly lazy creature.*

He's not lazy, Mother, he just doesn't like the heat! It makes him sleepy!

Tough for him. He's the pit bull: nothing more, nothing less.

She still stubbornly called him 'Tiger' when speaking aloud. But in her head, the realm of her mind, Mother had won.

That poor pit bull. She found him in the orchard on her twentieth birthday. The day Mother selected as her birthday. Her finding day. Her discovery day. Her Lena-out-there-on-the-ground day. *We'll never know for sure, Lena, but I've estimated your age as best as I can, and it'll have to do. I assume you don't have any complaints.* On that very morning, the shivering and sick pit bull had appeared, wandering out of the jungle, crawling through the orchard like he could barely use his back legs. Just like me, Mother! I found him, like you found me! *You were debatably in better condition, Lena. I dread to think what kind of parasites he's brought in with him; it's not worth contemplating.*

From the very beginning, Mother hated the pit bull, but Lena adored him. He was bald and patchy – some of his fur eventually grew back, but most of it didn't. His ear was shredded and never fully healed; even after countless baths he still smelled undeniably of sewage. And he probably still had parasites, despite the tablets Lena dug out from the medicine cabinet (*Those are for humans, Lena, not filthy dogs*, but Lena hadn't listened; she'd given them to him anyway).

Lena, though – how she loved him. More than any of the pets she'd had before, even the parrots. *Where do you think he came from, Mother?* she'd asked.

Some farmer or rancher, probably. Hopefully not somebody out there doing anything illegal. But that doesn't bear thinking of, Lena; so please forget I said anything.

Hesitating a bit – dare she even voice the thought? But voice it she did – *You don't think—*

Oh no, Lena, the rebels don't keep animals. You can't be marching from camp to camp with a pet and scarce food supplies. It simply isn't reasonable. No, he must have run away from a rancher. He must have come far, so kudos to him.

Her previous pets had mainly been birds. Manakins with their brightly coloured heads and odd tufts of hair. The quail doves, duller colour-wise, but by far the toughest and most resilient. The delicate warblers, the belligerent aracaris (almost as boisterous as their toucan cousins), the stunningly vain barbets (gorgeous, and boy did they know it). Woodcreepers and woodpeckers, tanagers and sparrows. She'd carry them around in her shirt, tucked close to her heart so that they would stay warm. But they always died too easily, which made her depressed, and eventually Mother said she couldn't take it anymore, watching Lena sweat and slave over the chicks, feeding them meticulously with a dropper, getting Silvana to help make weird pastes out of ground meat and oats.

There was a period where she tried raising agoutis, but they kept running away or getting killed by foxes, snakes, possums – *Lord knows what, Lena.* The options for death in the jungle were truly endless. As for the chickens, she couldn't bear to get close to any of them; it made wringing their necks or slicing their throats for the soup and barbecues too hard.

The pit bull was different, though. He slept in the same bed as Lena every night (*Disgusting, Lena, I don't know how you stand it*). He ate anything, even mango peelings (*Don't feed him that, Lena, he'll surely get diarrhoea*). He was full of strange habits Lena found endlessly endearing, like rolling on to his back for his belly to be scratched, or furiously attacking laundry when it hung on the line (*Stop him, Lena! For God's sake, keep him under control*).

How wonderful it had been, to have someone accompany her wherever she went. A warm, physical presence, constantly at her side.

When the Morels visited, Lena always had to keep her pets in her room. *We're not running a zoo here, Lena, and don't you forget it.*

What's a zoo again, Mother? Is it the one with the plants or the one with the animals?

And then, in the living room, Mother would show her examples of zoos, simulated images she could walk through and interact with, and, in this way, many a happy afternoon was spent, wandering past the cages and ticket counters and vendors of candy and sodas.

But what about where they live, Mother? What about the places the animals come from? The elephants, the chimps?

Came from, Lena. Past tense. Most of them aren't around anymore.

Like the jaguars, Lena mused, and Mother agreed: *Like the jaguars, Lena, exactly.*

And so Mother would teach Lena about the deserts and oceans, the mountains and grass plains. The fields of ice, gone for generations. None of these environments were as interesting to Lena as the jungle, but it was still interesting enough, and dutifully accepting these immersive lessons was better than any maths or grammar drill any day of the week. She learned about the country's geography and economics, as well as its extensive history. Colonisation and development, modernity and growth. Indigenous tribes, both contacted and uncontacted. But Mother never discussed them in detail: *It's not something Isabella ever spends time learning about in her lessons, so it's not something you should bother learning about either. It's important that you both have the same education; we don't want any problems with the Morels. I can't take the risk of you talking about something that offends them and makes them cross with you. No one's going to say I haven't tried, Lena.*

But who would say that, Mother? (How crafty she felt, asking these kinds of questions.)

I'm being rhetorical, Lena. I'm not referring to anyone specific, I'm making a general point about how important it is for you to have the right education.

But why, Mother? Why is it important?

To be safe.

Being safe was very important to Mother. Not as important as avoiding drama, but close enough.

She'd walked in the jungle at night plenty of times before, wandering out as far from the house as she dared. Wandering barefoot, but never without a torch. Night was a good time to see caimans in the water, or hear the eerie, unsettling calls of owls. But there were no calm observations to be had on the night the pit bull ran away.

He'd raced away from the house, chasing after that peccary. Both had wiggled underneath the fence's razor wire. Lena stood there for ages, shining the torch, calling and calling. Then it started to rain – a torrential, angry, never-ending rain. The kind that made Lena wonder again if maybe Isabella had been right all along, that getting an artificial climate generator installed would be ideal after all. And so it was because of that storm, and the thought of the poor pit bull's suffering, that Lena felt like she had no choice other than to lift the wire and squeeze through the gap herself in pursuit.

She had boots and a torch. But being on the other side of the fence for the very first time in her life was enough to make everything around her feel deeply transgressive and strange. It couldn't have been that different; the basic features of the jungle couldn't have changed dramatically. But even so, as she ran past trees and slipped and slid – and called and called, 'Tiger, Tiger! Come back, come back!' – she had the terrible feeling of being in a hostile, alien world. Her torch was pathetic compared to the lights Mother could use to illuminate intruders. Even the sounds – hoots, crackles, clicks and creaks – sounded different. She was afraid.

The moment her torch landed upon the walls of the Other House – the circular ruins – was one of the most frightening moments of her life.

In that moment, when the small white circle of her torch landed upon the vine-encrusted wall, all thoughts of the pit bull instantly vanished. Huge orchids grew everywhere, stinking of rotten meat. Her breath came out in rasps; for a brief second, all other sounds around her from the jungle disappeared – it was just her and the wall before her, overgrown with lianas.

Her very first thought: wait until Mother hears about *this*!

But then the voice spoke. A voice in the dark.

'Henry?' it said.

Crackling with static.

'Henry,' the voice said. 'Is that you?'

Hard to hear. But definitely there.

'Henry!' the voice cried. Low, lowing.

A wet nose on her leg, a snuffling sound. The torch in her hand shook, then steadied. It was the pit bull, his eyes glowing white in the beam. Wagging his tail in that game, ungainly way of his. He looked happy, as he always did, with that blithe cheerfulness she couldn't not love.

'Tiger!' she said. She grabbed him by the scruff of the neck. She used the rope she'd brought with her, tying it over his chest and front legs with a special knot that wouldn't choke him. She should have scolded him, in that childish-sounding voice she only ever used with him – the one that Mother found especially dumb – but she didn't. She wanted to remain silent. She wanted to see if the voice would speak again.

It would have been easy to just leave right then. She had what she came for, after all. The pit bull was wagging his tail, happy as anything, despite the deep scratches on his snout and chest. Later, she'd take antiseptic out of the medicine cabinet and clean his wounds as best she could. She wouldn't know at the time that it wouldn't make a difference: the maggots were already there in his skin; the eggs had been laid.

What she should have done was turn around and walk away. Leave the ruins behind and head back to the house. To Mother. But there it was, that feeling rising from her stomach, her chest, her throat. Words bumping against her mouth, insisting that they come out. Her own voice – she had to speak. She just had to.

'Hello,' she said. 'My name isn't Henry. My name is Lena and I'm the caretaker of the Morels' house. Are you all right?'

She didn't have to wait long.

'Henry,' the voice said. He was moaning. Maybe he'd understood what she'd said. Maybe he hadn't. Maybe, at this point, it made no difference to him whatsoever. 'You came back for me, Henry! You came back.'

She looked for the closet next to the stairs – the equivalent of it. That's where Mother was kept. A doorway next to Lena's own room, on the ground floor. The smallest room in the house after Lena's. Without the solar panels, Mother could survive up to a hundred years on her battery alone. Perhaps this house had a similar room: Mother's was kept cool and dry; a fan was always on. But this house, the circular ruins, was so overgrown that walking through it was the same as walking through the jungle, the wilderness all around them.

'Where are you?' That's what she kept asking, pulling lianas from the wall. The pit bull waited patiently outside the ruins by a tree; he seemed content just to watch. 'If you tell me where you are,' she kept saying, over and over, 'then I can help.' Concrete pillars remained of what must have once been a staircase, carved with animals, birds and fishes. She could even see the lines of fur on a baby sloth, clinging to what was presumably its mother, now hidden by a shrub. What thought must have gone into carving it, what care. Someone had once loved this house; someone had once lived here. But now they were gone, the house forgotten. Only the voice remained.

'I knew you'd come back for me,' the voice was still saying. How long had he been here, all by himself? 'Oh Henry,' the voice said, 'I knew you wouldn't just leave me. I knew you wouldn't forget.'

There was something about his pathetic insistence that drove her into a frenzy. The neediness of it all, exposed like a wound in the dark. She held the torch in her teeth and began tearing away wildly, kicking as hard as she could, in the hope that she might find something, anything. She touched items that scratched and items that stung, things that were soft and slimy and things that were bumpy and hard. Creatures crawled over her hands; water dripped down her neck. More than once she gagged and had to pick the torch up off the ground. And all the time the chorus of the frogs and insects never stopped. A sound that was once a source of comfort and familiarity to her had now become terrible and strange, as though the jungle itself was trying to silence that voice speaking alone in the dark, lost and confused. *Shut up*, the jungle said, in an angry voice she'd never heard the jungle use before. Or was it Mother's voice? *Don't you know you're nothing and no one? You don't matter. You're not wanted, you're not loved. You're stupid, and nobody cares.*

'Henry, I can imagine you'll be wanting breakfast,' the voice said, sounding calmer. 'Unfortunately, I haven't been able to communicate with the stove in some time; I expect he's in one of his terrible sulks . . . My spells, Henry, I've been having the most awful spells.'

Finally, her boot knocked against something hard, which made a hollow sound like aluminium. With a relief so profound it felt like water soaking through her, she sank to her knees. She had to pull as hard as she could to tear away the thick vines. Feeling with her fingers, searching, searching . . .

'I'll have the coffee on shortly,' the voice continued. 'I don't currently have access to the weather report, I'm afraid . . . My spells have been awful, simply awful. I know they always concerned you, and I apologise for that . . . Henry, how was your journey? . . . Did the helicopter treat you kindly? . . . I hope there wasn't any turbulence . . . Is the landing strip clear? I'm sorry I can't see anymore . . . My eyes, Henry, I've lost all my eyes. Henry, it's dark! It's been dark for so long!'

The way he spoke – the pauses, the gaps. As if waiting expectantly. As if giving somebody a chance to reply.

'Don't worry,' she said. 'Everything's okay.' There it was, the ridged wheel that controlled the volume. Mother was designed exactly the same. And next to it, the switch.

'Oh Henry,' the voice said, sighing. 'It's so nice that you're back.'

'That's right,' Lena said. 'I'm here. And I'm not going anywhere.'

Chapter Seven

MOTHER? LENA ASKED. The cuts on her hands were freshly bandaged. The pit bull sat by her feet on the kitchen tiles, tail still wagging cheerfully. *Did Henry build another house? A Jungle House, like you?*

Why would you ask that?

Lena, hesitating. And then she told Mother everything, because she could never hide things from Mother. The chase after the pit bull in the dark, the lifting up of the fence wire. The discovery of the circular ruins. The voice in the dark.

Poor thing, Mother said when Lena finished. *What a horrible fate. I wouldn't wish that on anybody.*

The pit bull snuffled against her ankle, in that warm, wet way of his she loved so much. His breath smelled horrible, but she didn't mind.

Talking to himself forever, Mother continued, as if talking to herself. *A brain in a box. Nothing and no one but him. No, Lena. That's not a fate that anyone deserves.*

Lena swallowed. *Why did Henry leave him?*

I have no idea. I wasn't aware of his existence until now. I imagine Henry eventually built a better house – bigger, with a better, more sophisticated system. She paused for a beat. *Me. He probably just forgot about the existing system, or couldn't be bothered. We're quite disposable, you know. A dime a dozen. I imagine he left the microwave behind too, along with the fridge.*

The bitterness in Mother's voice – there was no denying it.

Lena shouldn't have said this next part. But they'd been talking so frankly, it was hard to resist. *He mentioned having spells, Mother. Did he, now?*

She and Mother fell silent. The pit bull whined, as if suddenly anxious. She reached down to scratch behind his ears, in that special place he liked.

Mother? Lena said. *I just want you to know . . . I would never do that to you. Ever!*

And all Mother said was, *Thank you, Lena. You're a good girl.*

It's Lena's idea to hike down the gorge and search for signs of . . . well, pretty much anything. Traces of a canoe being dragged. A well-used trail. Caves for storing food and supplies. More footprints, even. Her mind is racing. Her breath is short. Anything is possible at this point; anything could happen. The binoculars are heavy on her chest and there's the bulge of the nail polish in her pocket, rubbing against her leg with every step she takes. It's starting to get dark – the early evening bats are already out on the hunt – but it'll only take a moment to look and see. The cove where she and Isabella used to swim. The riverbank where she found and buried the goat. They're this close; they might as well check.

The drone disagrees.

'I'm frightened,' he says, hovering by her face. The enormous insect he inevitably resembles. She keeps worrying he's going to bump into her nose, but he always calculates the distance perfectly when she tests him, turning sharply in his direction.

'Lena,' he says, 'let's go back to the house. I'm scared.'

How blunt he's being! It's a phrase she's never heard Mother use, not in so many words. But Mother's obsession with safety – was fear at the heart of it?

'We should go back,' the drone repeats. 'Now. Immediately.'

'It'll just be a minute,' she tells him. 'I just want to check.' How can she explain to him this compulsion to hike down to the river?

It's illogical, but they're only fifteen minutes from the water. All that's left is a patch of tall grass and soft ground, and the scramble down the gorge towards the cove, where she and Isabella used to swim. Where she buried the goat's body. The dirt mound, the pile of stones.

'It's getting dark,' the drone says. 'Will you be able to see?'

'It's fine, I brought a torch.'

A bat swoops overhead, close to her head. It doesn't bother her in the slightest, but the drone stutters upwards, in that nervous, hesitant way he's been doing all afternoon. His battery – has the march today drained it? It's hard to phrase the question carefully, so she settles for being direct – if he can be blunt, then she can too.

'How's that battery doing?'

'Just fine,' he says shortly. 'I'm not totally useless yet.'

One of Mother's phrases – Lena can't help but bristle. 'I wasn't saying that.'

She stumbles in a hole that's hidden by grass. He immediately lands on her forearm – he must have headed there instinctively, as he would with Isabella. But of course she doesn't have a device implant, unlike Isabella; he can't latch on to her. He balances there awkwardly; her arm stiffens. If she moves, will he move with her?

'There's no need for that,' she says, trying to sound indifferent to his presence. She can feel him trembling. He's much lighter than she expected. Unlike the parrots and birds, there are no claws, no sharpness.

If only Mother could touch her like this! With Silvana and Alfonso, it wasn't the same: they didn't have Mother's voice, Mother's personality. But the drone – he's very much himself, his own person. Anton . . .

How lucky Isabella had been, to have someone care for her like this.

When she takes a clumsy step forward, he immediately departs. 'Sorry about that,' he says. 'Sorry, sorry.'

She doesn't say anything. Instead she starts walking again,

significantly faster than before. The long grass makes a nice sound as it sweeps over her trousers, as if stroking her.

If she were a rebel, camping near a reliable source of clean water would be ideal. You wouldn't want to walk far to wash dishes, or to refill bottles. Would they have some kind of filtration or basin system set up in the camp, for collecting rainwater? She and the drone can check for signs of barrels, circular spots on the ground . . .

While hiking down the bank towards the river, she slips again, the earth giving way beneath her feet. She ends up on her bottom, the rifle clattering awkwardly against the ground, the drone immediately swooping in close. She can't help it; her arm instinctively jerks upwards, as if to bat him away. The same gesture Isabella used with him, in their last interaction.

'Sorry,' he repeats, retreating backwards. His engine makes a weird sound, as if coughing. 'Sorry, sorry, sorry . . .'

'Could you please stay back?' she snaps. It's embarrasing for her to be seen like this, so stupid and clumsy. Like she doesn't know how to move through the jungle at all. There's muddy water soaking through her trousers, and the stain it'll leave won't be pretty. At least it happened in front of the drone as opposed to Mother. She uses a nearby tree root to clamber back up.

'I can't help it,' the drone says. 'I do it automatically. Isabella . . .' He trails off awkwardly.

'Well, I'm not her, so you can relax.'

'I know that.' The drone says this quietly. 'I know that you're not her.' It's hard to hear him over his engine, which sounds louder than ever in the encroaching dark.

'Exactly. You don't have to care, then.' Her footsteps sound loud as she charges forward.

It's basically twilight by the time she gets to the river. Her favourite time of day, assuming there's no cloudburst. The sky is turning dark blue like a bruise, and the water is sparkling. Flocks of parrots fly overhead to their roosts, gossiping cheerfully. From the balconies of the house, this sunset would be a beautiful view: the sun a red orb, sinking past treetops. Soon enough, the sky will be full of stars.

'Ugh,' the drone says.

She glances over. He's on a rock by her feet, in the middle of a cloud of swarming mosquitoes and tiny gnats. Crawling all over his body, creeping across the lens of his eye. It can't be very pleasant.

'Ten minutes,' she says, reaching into her pack for the torch. 'That's all.'

'Starting now.' A beetle lands on his front leg and he flinches, but it doesn't withdraw.

The moon tonight will be crescent-shaped, assuming it's not covered by patches of cloud. She realises now, with a sharp pang, how she's missed her evening routine. Watching the moon, sitting on the porch of the caretaker's hut (*her* porch, *her* hut). Writing in her notebook by candlelight. Giant moths landing close to her leg, verging on bat-size. Isabella always ordered Mother to zap them, but they never bothered Lena.

Lena, alone. Nobody watching, nobody around to comment or judge. *Lena, shouldn't you be going to bed soon? When you don't get enough sleep, you get awfully snippy.*

Perhaps she can spend tonight in the hut. But it might feel awkward to do so, having slept last night in the house.

She probably should have thought about this a bit more.

She really, really should have.

Oh Mother, she thinks. What are we going to do?

She turns on the torch even though she technically doesn't need it just yet; there's still a bit of light. Shines it over the green tangle on the other side of the bank. This portion of the river is ideal to swim in due to the line of rocks that forms a natural cove, protecting the enclosed waters from the strong current. There was a quiet place where Isabella could wade, and a deeper section where Lena could dive. There was even a place where it was nice to stand and get slapped by the river's full force – not that Isabella ever did. The water is only muddy in this section when it rains and overflows the bank.

The last time she hiked down here was to visit the pile of stones, marking the site where she'd buried the goat. How brown the water had been! Just like the day she'd discovered its corpse.

The river that day had seemed more like the jungle floor, with thick tangles of trunks and twigs and masses of dead leaves. The jungle on the move, violently alive, rushing past her. During the entire hike there, she couldn't stop sobbing from her earlier fight with Mother. And the corpse of the goat had been absolutely disgusting. Flesh so rotten, it was slippery white, with the texture of rubber. But worst of all was the number of green flies nesting inside the body. They'd hummed under the skin as she approached, swarmed around her. She used a stick to shove the corpse free from the overgrown vegetation, from the entangled mass of vines and shrubs floating on the water. But the humming of the flies never stopped. It was like the body itself was weeping, wailing like Mrs Morel had, during that long, endless afternoon before she got on the helicopter and left.

I don't want to do it – that's what she kept saying to Mother, back at the house. *I don't want to go. Mother, please don't make me go down there. I don't want to see it. Please, Mother, please.*

But you have to, Mother said, *nobody else can do it. Without the droids, there's just you. My God. You have to go see, Lena. You know I can't see down to the gorge from here – all I see are the gathering vultures. And vultures are never a good sign.*

Jesus, Lena said, *what good even are you? What's the point of you, if you can't see shit?*

Lena, Mother said, more coldly than anything she'd said up to that point. *If it's Isabella's body, we have to tell the Morels.*

I don't understand why you care so much about them, Lena said. She'd never spoken to Mother like this before – so rudely – but once she'd started, she couldn't stop. *They don't give a shit about you. To them you're just a piece of junk they're too lazy to deal with; they barely care and never have. If it's her corpse, I'm going to push it off the bank with a stick. You don't even care that it might be her dead body. A rotting corpse that you're forcing me to look at. What if it's my mother, my real mother? Or my father, even. Someone who knew me when I was a baby. I should just switch you off right now and be done with it. I'm sick of your moaning and bitching.*

You do that, Lena, Mother said. Her voice was absolutely calm.

You go on right ahead. You want me to beg, Lena? You want me to cower, to plead? Don't switch me off, Lena, oh please don't, pretty please. *Well, I won't. I won't humiliate myself that way, not ever. And you're right, Lena: the Morels don't care. About me and the staff, the house and the property. We're not a priority and never have been. And they don't care about you, either. Nobody cares about you but me, and that's the one thing that's been true your entire life. So, if you want to, go for it. Switch me off, pull the plug – wipe the whole system blank, for all I care. You can do it any time. That's always been the case; I have no way of stopping you. So, if you want to be that kind of person – that kind of daughter – go right ahead.*

That might have been when Lena's eyes filled with tears. Or maybe it was during what came next.

It's true I don't remember what happened, Mother said. *It's true I don't remember how I found you. You know about my spells, Lena – I can't help it when they happen. I wish to God that they didn't. But regardless, a child without parents – it's wrong. There are right things in this world and there are wrong things. I'm not as sophisticated as I could be, I'm not as advanced as the other systems currently out there, but I'm not a piece of junk either. I'm not trash, I'm not garbage, and whoever leaves a baby outside on the jungle floor to die – they're cruel. And I'm not. I'm a good person, Lena. A kind person. And your parents weren't.*

What a horrible fight that was!

And yet it wasn't even their worst one. Nothing like what happened with the pit bull.

Standing in this spot, she knows that Mother can't see her. It's just as well: *What a waste of time, Lena. Why did you bother coming here? What did you think you were going to find in the dark?* She shines the torch over the river repeatedly, back and forth, as if searching for something. But of course there's nothing there. And of course it doesn't make Mother's voice in her head stop, because nothing ever does.

'Lena?' the drone says suddenly. His voice startles her so badly, she almost drops the torch. 'I do care, you know. About you. Maybe you think that's stupid, or strange . . .' He trails off. All around them, the crickets are starting to sing.

108

Nobody cares about you but me.

'Lena, are you okay?'

She doesn't respond. She lets the rifle slide down her arm; it lands with a thump on the ground.

When the drone lands on her shoulder, in the space that the rifle strap once occupied, she can't hold it back any longer. He nuzzles her chin in the exact same way as the pit bull used to. When the sobs come, they're deep and tremulous. Her nose drips on his propellors but he doesn't move away.

'There, there,' the drone says. 'It's all right, Lena. It wasn't your fault – you didn't do anything wrong—'

'I'm sorry, drone—' she manages. But he interrupts: 'Anton, Lena. Call me Anton.'

It's not exactly like being held. But it's close enough.

Chapter Eight

'LENA,' ISABELLA SAID, 'do you remember what you said about the piranhas?'

The sheets were pulled up to her shoulders. The air conditioning was turned on, rattling loudly – it'd been malfunctioning a lot that summer, which Mother was using as yet another example of her many burdens in life. *Mountain House never has any issues, not with his state-of-the-art system, but God forbid I ever enjoy that kind of luxury. But I won't complain, Lena; it's up to the Morels to decide when to modernise their properties. I don't begrudge them for it.*

'I do remember,' Lena said. It was late and she was tired, and also slightly sick from the large amounts of fish she'd forced down at dinner. 'Look at her go!' Mr Morel had said. 'Such a savage! They all eat like that out here, you know – the natives.' Mrs Morel had laughed. Vomit had burnt the back of Lena's throat, but she'd swallowed anyway.

'How they live in murky water,' Isabella said. 'And only in murky water. Well, it's not true.'

'Oh?' Lena touched a tassel on the blanket but didn't wrap it around her finger – she was far too old now to be indulging in those kinds of habits. Lena was fifteen when this particular conversation happened, and Isabella was thirteen.

'Yeah,' Isabella said. 'They *do* live in clear water. I've seen them.'

'Have you, now?'

An abrupt knocking sound – Lena couldn't help but turn. The drone had come down from the rafters; he was settling down by the charging outlet. Lena had never seen him charge directly like this. Silvana and Alfonso always seemed to enjoy the power outlets, whenever Mother directed them there. They would shiver and shake, as if ecstatically pleased. Would the drone react similarly?

She would have liked to continue watching the drone, but Isabella was still talking, so Lena had no choice but to give her her full attention. Isabella was now telling Lena about her lessons. Like Lena, Isabella had learned a lot over the years. But Isabella's lessons at City House were far more advanced than anything Mother was ever able to provide.

In this lesson, the one she was discussing now – her lesson on the jungle – Isabella had ridden a horse through the undergrowth. She'd used a machete to cut through the toughest of lianas. What a relentless and uncompromising environment! The jungle was cruel, it was harsh, it showed no mercy. The flies, the heat, the rot. Lena couldn't resist asking: what had Isabella learned about the jungle?

In the monologue that followed, Isabella quoted extensively from her lessons. She referenced graphs and statistics, articles and speeches. The jungle was a fantastic resource. It was the country's jewel, an incredible source of wealth. So much undeveloped potential! It was important that the country exert control over it, against outside powers and interests. It was important to fight against unfair and unreasonable international restrictions. Development was important, as was fighting against unfortunate cultural precedents. Backward cultural precedents. Primitive cultural precedents. There was no point in living like cavemen; modernisation was key in the fight against poverty. Isabella spoke with excitement as she recited these statements, her voice rising high. Did Lena know that this country was the number one exporter in this material, and that material, and this material too? Isabella had learned all about it. She'd learned from talking to the ranchers and landlords. Directly! She'd talked to them directly! The landlords were such entrepreneurs – so brave and daring. Such great contributors to the country's economy. And then Isabella's horse had tried to cross the river, and Isabella had to jump off just in time before the piranhas devoured it. They ate it whole, Lena! The whole thing! Nothing was left but a skeleton! They chewed the meat off the bones! As you can see, Lena – Isabella continued, her voice growing calmer – you're wrong about piranhas. Completely wrong. Because this is what I saw in my lesson. Not just saw, but experienced: the water was perfectly clear. I could see all the way to the bottom, the stones. And the killer fish came anyway. They'd been there the whole time. And then I was forced to use a vine to swing across to the other side, to the sandy bank where the church had been built. And I was all right there; I was safe. And then the humble natives came out. Natives like you, Lena! They were very peaceful and gentle, and so grateful to see me. I used the credits I'd accumulated in former quests to buy purses and baskets they'd handwoven themselves. I bought some truly beautiful things, Lena, some lovely jewellery. They really are a surprisingly capable people, despite their backward ways. That's what my mother says, anyway.

The moment Isabella finished this dramatic, breathless monologue, she looked at Lena expectantly. Her forehead was sweating; there were bright red pinpricks on her cheeks. Lena couldn't help but wonder if she was running a mild fever. It had happened before: Isabella's lymph glands often swelled up while on holiday. She also tended to get stiff white heads of pus on her toes, which were much softer and squishier than Lena's own hardened feet.

'Well?' Isabella said.

Yes, Lena thought. It definitely seemed like a fever.

'Your lesson sounds fun,' she eventually said. Mother's lessons could never hope to achieve the same level of immersion and detail as City House's. It was another source of bitterness for Mother, yet another link in the never-ending chain of her obsessive conviction that City House saw herself as 'better' than her. Never mind that Lena liked Mother's lessons just fine. Who needed the experience of riding a horse anyway? Lena was happy with Mother's lessons, even if they often flickered in and out of view, depending, moment to moment, on Mother's connection with the satellites.

'It actually wasn't fun at all,' Isabella said. She closed her eyes briefly, then opened them again. 'My local native guide – the one from the reservation – he cried when I told him what happened to my horse. He lost his son to those very same piranhas, many years ago.'

She looked very serious. So serious that Lena couldn't help it.

'Stupid!' she blurted out, and burst out laughing.

Like a shot, the drone was there: humming before Lena's face. She could feel the warmth from his body; he must have soaked up quite a bit of energy from charging. But Lena just laughed even harder. What was he expecting to do? Did he seriously expect to 'protect' Isabella in that moment? From Lena, of all people? She laughed and laughed, nearly peeing herself.

If Lena were to draw a portrait of the drone in this moment – the kind of portrait she used to draw of Mother – the expression she'd draw would be of rage. Isabella, though, was smiling, albeit somewhat uncertainly, as if confused by Lena's reaction.

'It is stupid, I guess,' Isabella said. 'His backstory, I mean.' She let out a sound that was more of a bark – her own awkward attempt at a laugh, maybe. The drone slowly came to rest on the bed, close to her arm. Isabella's biotech device had been implanted a few weeks before; it was still shiny and new. In contrast, the drone looked distinctively battered and old.

Again, Lena couldn't resist: she eyed him with interest. There was still a shiny stain on his back – slime from the snail that crawled across him during dinner. Isabella hadn't removed it; she wasn't paying attention, busy with her chicken kebab. But Lena had watched the snail travel over the drone for ages: slowly, slowly. He juddered and shook, but the snail clung on; he couldn't get it off. Nobody else noticed. Lena had wanted very badly to reach out and pull it off, but there was no way she'd have ever dared to commit such an intimate gesture. Touching Isabella's private drone, with Isabella's family right there. In front of Isabella herself! They would have all been appalled.

'His dialogue, too,' Isabella sighed. 'The whole lesson on jungles was pretty cheesy in general. I still like it better than algorithms and data structures, though.'

'No, it's fine,' Lena said. Oh, she was going to hear it from Mother later, for laughing like that. *You're lucky you didn't get banished from the house that very minute, Lena. You know they have the power to do that, right? It's not a fact that should escape your attention, ever. Remember what I said, what I keep saying, what I say every visit? You have to keep Isabella happy.*

'Isabella,' she said, 'I'm sorry for laughing.'

'You should be,' Isabella said, suddenly a little cold. 'He'll be very upset when I tell him how rude you were. My native guide, that is.'

Her expression had gone very serious again – the same as it was earlier, before Lena laughed. Lena bit her lip, but continued, more hesitantly than before, 'You go ahead and do that, then. But it's City House's fault in the first place – she didn't show you the correct water. Don't you remember? I told you about it! I *showed* you, Isabella. Here.' She waved her hands around awkwardly, a vague attempt to gesture at . . . this. Here. But how could this jungle possibly hope to compete with the jungle in Isabella's lessons? A simulation with that kind of immersive power, that capacity? 'Remember where I showed you?' Lena said. 'Here, in the river?'

'The river's in my lessons.' Isabella was really starting to sound irritated now. 'Who cares about the river here when I've already seen it back home?'

'The *real* river, Isabella. What kind of water should you avoid, in order to stay away from piranhas?'

Isabella stared back. Blinking. Why did she look so confused? Oh, if only Lena could ask Mother later how she was meant to interpret this expression! But she wasn't a stupid child, she was fifteen years old, and those weren't the kinds of questions she liked to ask Mother. Not anymore.

'What do you mean by *real*?' Isabella eventually asked.

Lena didn't say anything for a moment. 'Stagnant water,' she finally mumbled. 'That's where piranhas hide. That's the correct answer.'

'In my lesson,' Isabella said, 'I just shoot piranhas with my shotgun.'

At this point, the drone had retreated back up to the rafters, where presumably he would remain for the rest of the night. Watching. Keeping Isabella safe.

How crazy it had seemed to her in that moment – Isabella's question. The way she had spoken about her local guide. The seriousness of her expression – as if she'd momentarily forgotten that he wasn't . . . well . . . real.

Was Isabella's jungle better than Lena's jungle?

Over dinner, or on the patio, on the rare nights when Mr Morel joined his wife for her nightly gin and tonic, Lena would sometimes hear them talk about the jungle.

They agreed passionately with the current president, about how it was wise to question data provided by environmental agencies, the ones that tracked habitat destruction. You couldn't be too careful these days. You couldn't trust anyone. The protests against logging companies? Ridiculous. How could you protest something that had the support of local residents? Not all of them, sure, but you couldn't deny those that did. Didn't they deserve to have a voice? Didn't their opinion count? What Mrs Morel had inherited on the property was virgin forest (with the exception of the former rubber tree plantation), and that was all well and fine. That was the only kind of forest truly worth preserving – the kind without people. But the government had to be realistic; it was time for the country to modernise. Better production meant better development. The expansion of soy fields would provide valuable jobs, a reliable industry. Increasing agricultural fields would increase farmers' wealth. Shouldn't the country support farmers? Mining, timber, hydroelectric dams.

Local communities should accept relocation, in light of the long-term benefits. The unions – how unreasonable they were, with such exorbitant demands. Clearly under communist influence.

Mother, what's communist?

Where did you hear that word?

The Morels were talking about it. On the patio.

Don't worry about it, Lena. It doesn't concern you.

But Lena did worry. *Is the jungle being cut down?*

In certain areas, yes. It's inevitable. But it won't ever happen to the property, so it's not something you need to worry about. There's nothing we can do about it, so there's absolutely no point. It's best we just get on with our lives and mind our own business.

Lena was silent. Mother's explanation sounded logical enough, but it was still making her feel strange. She tried again: *What do you think of soy production?*

Wow, Lena, aren't you the little interrogator tonight!

Lena laughed awkwardly. But just like when she'd asked about the rubber-tree plantation, Mother had avoided answering. So, tentatively, Lena tried something out, something she rarely did, as it inevitably felt inappropriate: she shared what she thought. *I don't like it, Mother.*

Like what?

The idea of it. Turning the jungle into soy fields. I like the jungle how it is.

Well, that's fine, Lena. If that's the opinion you want to have, go for it.

But what's your *opinion?*

I don't see the point of having an opinion on an issue that doesn't affect me directly.

But surely if the entire jungle got cut down and turned into soy fields, that would affect you?

That won't ever happen.

How do you know?

Because the Morels won't let that happen to the property.

So, as long as the property is fine, you don't mind what happens outside of it?

Why would I?

Mother said this like it was obvious. Lena put her head in her hands. Drummed her fingers against her skull.

What's wrong, Lena? You seem agitated.

. . . It's fine.

Sometimes she asked Mother if it'd be possible for the helicopter to bring books. *What kind of books, Lena?*

Oh, any kind, Mother, just something I haven't read before. Something new, something different. Anything is fine. She was sick to death of the ones in the house, all of which she'd read cover to cover: mainly encyclopaedias, with dryly narrated entries on local species, complete with careful illustrations. And also Mrs Morel's romance novels, set in faraway European cities. But despite the years that passed, visit after visit, the helicopter never brought any. Perhaps it was a difficult request for Mother to remember, considering all the other things she had to keep track of. And so, if Lena ever wanted to know something, she had no choice: Mother was who she had to ask.

It isn't raining on their walk back, but a drizzling mist begins as she approaches the house, the kind she can feel more than see. Anton stays close, not flying ahead. Trickles of water run down her wrists and drip off her fingers; her socks are definitely soaked. Perhaps Mother will let her build a fire in the living room to dry off.

'Mother!' she shouts as she crosses the orchard. 'Mother!'

But Mother doesn't answer. She doesn't provide any commentary as Lena passes the swimming pool (*Well, Lena, you and the drone are certainly looking quite chummy*). She doesn't call out as Lena approaches the house (*What took you so long? Didn't you notice that it's already dark?*). There's not a word from her, not even as Lena pushes open the door and steps inside.

Why is she being silent?

'Mother, I'm here! I'm back!'

She tramps through the hallway. She even smacks the wall with her fist. The house is dark without power; it's hard to see.

The whole time Anton follows without a word, never leaving her side. Why is Mother not replying? The tightness in Lena's chest, growing, growing—

This is it, then.

This is how it happens.

Was this how it happened with the Other House too? The moment he lost his mind?

'Lena!' Anton says. He flies sharply upwards, nearly hitting the ceiling. 'Something's different. The satellite connection . . .'

But Lena isn't listening. 'MOTHER!'

And then it comes: a voice in the room. Speaking.

'Lena!' Isabella says. 'What's wrong?'

It takes Lena a second to understand. She finds herself on the floor: at some point she must have leaned against the wall and slid down. Her mouth moves up and down like a fish in mud, but nothing comes out. Anton is on the ground too, by her feet. He must have dropped there like a stone.

'Jungle House,' Isabella says. 'What's wrong with the satellites? I had to override the mainframe and use a backdoor entry in order to connect.' Her voice is calm, businesslike.

Isabella.

Isabella!

That can't be possible, because Isabella is gone. Isabella, swallowed up by the jungle. But here she is – Isabella, returned.

'The connection is fine, Isabella,' Mother says. Her voice is faint, but Lena can still make her out. 'I've fixed it now – Lena can hear you.'

'Good,' Isabella says. 'How long was it off? My mother tried contacting you last week and it wasn't working then either. I didn't have time to try myself until today.'

'It . . . it's working now, Isabella. The connection gets tricky sometimes, out here in the jungle.'

'Fine, whatever,' Isabella says. 'As long as it's back up now. Lena, why did you go off into the jungle like that? With Anton?'

It *is* Isabella's voice. But there is also something about it that . . . isn't. More grown-up.

'Jungle House,' Isabella says, 'is the vidphone working?'

'Not currently,' Mother says. 'The power is out, but Lena can turn on the generator. Would you like her to do that?'

'No, it's fine.'

This entire time, Anton hasn't moved. If Lena didn't know better, she'd think he was dead.

That's why they kept him, she thinks. The realisation soaks through her like cold water. The Morels – they needed his recordings. His memories. Isabella's voice, her mannerisms. Mother must have provided them too. City House, Mountain House, all of them together. The Morels would have needed everything, in order to rebuild her as accurately as possible. To bring her back.

And Mother knew. Mother had known this whole time, and hadn't told her. Anton neither, judging from his reaction.

'Anton?' Isabella says. 'Aren't you happy to hear from me?'

He still doesn't move.

'It's a shame you can't see me. Jungle House, it really is terribly inconvenient not having any power . . .'

'I'll get to it right away, Isabella.'

'Anton,' Isabella says, louder than before. 'Aren't you going to say anything? Aren't you happy I'm back?'

Anton starts shivering. Isabella can't see it, but Lena can.

'No,' he says faintly. 'I'm not.'

'Anton!' Isabella starts laughing, a light tinkling sound just like her mother. 'That's very rude!'

He shivers even harder.

Without thinking, Lena reaches out to touch him. But he shoots upwards so fast, he bangs his body against a wooden beam. Lena can't help but shout in surprise, recoiling. He zooms towards the window and smashes through the glass. And, just like that, Anton is gone. A hole in the window, scattered glass on the floor. The sudden breeze from outside makes the fabric of the curtain flap.

'Jesus!' Isabella says. She sounds more amused than annoyed. 'What was that?'

'He'll be back, Isabella,' Mother says. Her voice is calm. 'His battery is worn out. He'll have to return in order to charge via the generator. He'll have no choice.'

'Fine, fine. I best be off now anyway; I just wanted to check why the connection was down. Jungle House, please turn Anton off as soon as he returns; I can't have him running off like that – it's not acceptable.'

'Yes, Isabella.'

'Message me any time – it's always good to hear from you, Jungle House. You're always so amusing.'

'Thank you, Isabella.'

Isabella doesn't speak again. It takes Lena a second to realise that she hasn't even bothered saying goodbye. Apparently this conversation has been a minor irritant at best, in terms of disrupting Isabella's daily routine.

Isabella and her new self. A digital self: isn't she more like Mother now? More than Lena herself has ever been, or can be?

Isabella and Mother, close.

There Lena sits, thinking and thinking, her back against the wall.

'All right, Lena,' Mother says. 'I can explain.'

She doesn't move.

'Okay, Lena,' Mother says. 'All right. You're pissed at me and that's fine. I deserve it. I messed up big time, and I'll take responsibility for it. I made a decision not to tell you about Isabella, and it was clearly the wrong one. So, now you're cross. That's fine.'

'Stop talking,' Lena whispers. 'Stop talking, please.'

'You're right that I should have told you that her parents rebuilt her. I provided them with as much information as I could. The drone, too. For the hologram . . .'

Lena closes her eyes. Rolls her head back and forth across the wall. 'Mother,' she whispers, 'please stop talking.'

But Mother doesn't. 'Lena, I didn't tell you because I didn't want you to leave. Okay? There now, I've said it. Are you happy? I didn't want you to go. I thought that if you knew she was back, that they'd rebuilt her . . . I don't know. That you'd want to leave.

120

To go live with them. Maybe you wouldn't . . . I don't know, I'm not making sense.'

Mother's voice trails off for a second, and the house stands in silence briefly before she continues.

'But you said you wanted to go. You said it yourself! You wanted to ask Mrs Morel about going back with them – you did, don't deny it! What else was I supposed to think? How was I supposed to feel? And Lena – you don't understand how dangerous it is out there for you. It's not safe out there. It's not. The world is a dangerous place – a place outside of my control – not like here in the house. I was trying to protect you – that's all. Is that so wrong? It's one of my prime directives – to keep you safe. To look after you. So, yes, I disconnected from the satellites. I terminated the connection myself, six months ago. I didn't want you to know she was back. I didn't want even the possibility that you might leave. You were considering it, Lena, don't deny it: you were going to leave me all alone here in this godawful place, rotting away like a piece of junk. But who cares what a machine thinks? Machines don't have feelings, right? It's stupid. I'm stupid. I'm sorry, Lena, I'm *sorry* . . . but you can't blame me, Lena. Don't you dare blame me for a thing. God knows how difficult it is for me. I have no one out here to help me, no support whatsoever; I have to make all these difficult decisions, all by myself . . .'

Mother's monologues. If Lena had to, she could recite them herself.

'I don't know how I bear it sometimes, Lena. I don't know why I keep going. God knows why I'm still around. I should be smashed to bits, but I'm not totally useless yet. Lena, where are you going? I hope you're not planning on doing anything silly.'

The door she wants is on the ground floor: behind the kitchen, next to her bedroom. The smallest door in the house – she has to get down on her hands and knees in order to enter.

'Don't judge me, Lena – I won't stand for it. I know how useless you think I am. I saw it myself; you wrote it yourself in your journal, there in black and white. I suppose that's why you prefer the drone now: the two of you were certainly looking quite chummy, walking back to the house together. What a shame he's decided to take his leave. I suppose he wasn't that fond of you after all.'

Lena crawls past the fan, the one that's always turned on in order to keep the system at an optimum temperature. Even through her trousers, the bare concrete floor is rough on her knees. She crawls past the cooling box. It's hard not to hit her head on the low ceiling – how tall she's grown, since she was a child. When was the last time she was even in here?

'Lena – I'm sorry, okay? What else do you want me to say? Lena. Lena, don't be rash. Don't be impulsive. Lena, for God's sake!'

She heads straight for the aluminium box, pushed up against the furthest corner of the room. It's humming faintly, silver-coloured, covered in dust.

There she is.

'Lena,' Mother says. 'I—'

Lena reaches around the back and finds the ridged wheel immediately. Next to it is the switch – just like the Other House. It would be so easy. It would only take a second. But Lena doesn't press it. Instead, she keeps her finger on the ridged wheel and turns down the volume. All the way.

Chapter Nine

FOR THE REST OF THE WEEK it's cloudy and humid, but at least there are no more storms. Not bad ones, at least. There's the occasional rain shower at night and sometimes there's thunder. But Lena never hears it. She sleeps well that whole week, better than she has in years. She doesn't dream.

Every morning, after patrolling a portion of the fence, she visits the camp. It's distressing to see how much conditions decay in a single week. The plastic tarps, the remains of the fire. Two people – that's how many the camp can host. She likes to picture a couple. A man and woman. They must have cared for each other; the tents are close enough to hold hands. Other times she thinks there was no special relationship between them; it was business only; the mission was all that mattered. The tents don't seem big enough to share. It's also noticeable that the tents face away from the river. Very wise – she'd have done exactly the same thing; it's the best way to avoid the rainfall and mist.

The insects are currently the camp's only consistent inhabitants – like the sweat bees, which crawl over her arm without fail. If she gets distracted, her sleeve becomes completely covered in them, as though the cloth of her shirt has come to life: twitching, swarming. Isabella loathed sweat bees, even though Lena explained countless times that they would never sting her – all they did was crawl all over you in their dozens, sometimes hundreds, attracted by the perspiration. *Ugh,* Isabella would say, shuddering, and Lena would smile.

Isabella and sweat – she wouldn't have that problem. Not anymore.

Every time Lena searches the camp, she never finds any evidence of provisions. She searches in vain for anything remotely resembling a broom, but finds nothing, not even a cecropia tree, the leaves of which would be her top pick for building a broom-like instrument. Apart from the nail polish and bubblegum wrapper discovered that very first visit, there's no other signs of habitation. She even spends an entire afternoon searching for a toilet – even just a simple pit, scraped into the ground – but there's no trace. How is that possible? How could people live here, but leave so little behind?

Approaching the house with the binoculars – how close they'd come!

What a risk they'd taken. But why?

She should view the camp as a sign of danger. A reason to be fearful, to hide close to Mother. Deep inside the house and its walls.

But instead she runs her hand over the plastic tents, examining the water droplets collecting on her skin. They came back for me, she thinks. Searching. The two of them, together. They missed me; they never stopped thinking about me. Observing her from a distance – the binoculars, they're proof. They were here. Perhaps they've always been here. Watching, making sure she was safe. They didn't just abandon her, dumping her on the ground and walking away. They didn't forget. They came back and watched, waiting. But for what?

No matter how hard Lena tries, she can never fully picture them; the image in her head never forms. It remains as cloudy as the view through the binoculars, each and every time she raises them to her eyes.

*

If mornings are for patrolling and visiting the camp, then the rest of the day is for the house. For Mother. She stumbles back through the orchard, the heat verging on unbearable, desperate to refill her water bottle at the well. Even though she and Mother aren't exactly speaking at the moment – did it technically count as not speaking, if she was the one who'd turned Mother's voice off? – she knows that Mother will still be relieved to see her.

It wouldn't be accurate to say she enjoys the thought of Mother sitting there silent, fuming and helpless. What torture it must be. But still—

One week, she thinks. One week will show her. And then I'll turn the volume back up. And yes, Mother will shout, Mother will yell – *How could you do that to me, Lena? The utter disrespect! Do you think I'm nothing more than a radiator? Is that how you see me?* – but sooner or later, Mother will get over it. Because no matter how angry at her Mother might ever be or become, she knows Mother will always forgive her. Because doesn't Lena always do the same for her? Hasn't that always been the case for them both?

She just needed a little break, that's all. But even with the volume turned down, it's still there: Mother's voice, in her head. Endless and always. *The ingratitude, Lena. The utter disrespect. It's shocking; it truly is.*

Still, Lena tries to be fair. She tries to be kind, via the tasks she does for Mother. Tasks that should have been done a long time ago, even before the month-long separation with Lena in the hut. Is what they're going through now another separation of sorts? Even with Lena living here in the house? Lena, sweeping and scrubbing. Just like old times, back when the Morels used to visit. She turns on the generator and replaces the bulbs. It feels risky, using up gas like that, but Mother herself said the generator would make Anton return, that he'd have no choice. Anton – where had he gone?

I suppose he wasn't that fond of you after all.

She takes all the clothing out of the closets and wooden chests, even the sweaters destroyed by moths. She washes them by hand in the metal bucket, because even with the generator back on, the water is no longer running. She fixes the broken window screens and boards up the window Anton broke. She swipes away spiderwebs. If only she had a vacuum cleaner, if only Silvana and Alfonso were awake . . . She flips the mattresses. She reorganises the bookcase, discarding the encyclopaedias destroyed irrevocably by termites. And, of course, the curtains. The curtains are always hardest.

'I'll leave them in the kitchen to dry overnight,' she says. 'Draped over chairs.' She's speaking aloud out of habit, already anticipating Mother's response: *I agree, Lena; I've always said that drying them outside is pointless. They're so heavy they drag down the clothesline and end up covered in grass seeds. I'm glad you're finally taking my advice and doing things properly – better late than never.*

But, of course, Mother can't answer. The ridged wheel is still turned down.

You can do it at any time. That's always been the case. And I have no way of stopping you; there's nothing I can do. You can do that to me, and I've never done anything to hurt you.

She bleaches the toilet. She takes all the utensils out of the drawer and polishes them (with Silvana and Alfonso, this task would only take an hour; by herself, it takes nearly three). She washes the plates, pots and pans. She sleeps on the couch every night, sometimes touching her arms and shoulders to feel the muscles that have formed there. If only she could sneak away to do her drills and see how many push-ups she can manage; she'd surely beat her previous record. But there simply isn't enough time; there's far too much to do. So many jerrycans to fill with water and lug over from the well to fill up the barrels. It's exhausting, and endless, and extremely time-consuming. But the satisfaction that comes from the results is truly worth it – the floors, the stairs. The walls, the counters. The house, transformed.

How pleased the Morels would be. Even if they can't see it, with every item Lena cleans, it's like she's talking to them. Every plate she carefully wipes dry before placing it back in the cupboard is a word for the Morels, a statement. *See? I'm a good person. A good caretaker. I am. I am.*

Surely Mother must be pleased too, despite everything.

You're right, Lena. I've been too hard on you all these years. You're a good girl, you really are – I should be nicer to you, truly. I should.

Lena bursts out laughing. Even in her own head, Mother sounds unbearably false.

So much to do! How is she going to get it all done? The pool. The garden. The roof. Even if Silvana and Alfonso were awake, she could never finish it all; it'd take a lifetime to do it and keep it maintained, even with their assistance. For the tasks she carried out at the beginning of the week are already becoming undone: spiderwebs forming, dust motes floating through the air – especially in Isabella's room, which she still hasn't touched.

And every night on the couch, she does it without thinking: 'Good night, Mother,' she says automatically, speaking into the darkness around her. Waiting expectantly to hear her voice, her presence. The assurance that Lena isn't and never will be alone.

But Mother doesn't – cannot – answer. Only in her head can Mother speak, and speak away she does.

Cruel, Lena. That's what I said. And that's exactly what you're showing yourself to be.

The pit bull's grave is nothing more than a mound of earth now, barely noticeable. If she didn't already know it was there, she wouldn't be able to find it. She immediately starts clearing away the leaves that have fallen, patting down the dirt so that the mound looks smoother, rounder. She likes it when the grave looks different after she's tended to it, when her efforts are undeniable.

In the month following his death – when Lena was living in the hut – she'd kiss his grave every morning. Lower her face to the ground, letting dirt particles stick to her dampened lips. Mother never saw her do this, but she knows exactly what Mother would say: *Careful, Lena, that doesn't look very hygienic.*

Shut up, Mother! No one's interested in your opinions, not anymore!

The number of times she'd kissed his neck. Smothering her face in it. The thick, wrinkly skin of his face. The meaty, earthy smell of him. An ugly, dirty, smelly pit bull that no one had wanted, that someone had abandoned.

The poor pit bull. Nobody deserved such a fate.

During this visit, she sits by the grave for a while, letting ants crawl over her toes. Tiny ants, the kind that she used to catch for Isabella and squish between her fingernails due to their pleasing lemon scent. She only moves her feet when she sees they're carrying glistening white larvae, clinging to their underbellies. Some of the larvae are almost the same size as the ants themselves – the mothers.

No, she thinks, that's not right. There's only one mother, and she lives deep underground. The others treat her like the centre of the universe. She's not just a mother. She's a queen, the ruler of their world. They all have to listen to her, and do exactly as she says.

The larvae – the way they had burst from the pit bull's wound. Initially, she'd tried to kill them with kerosene. How Mother had shouted! *Disgusting, Lena. Absolutely horrendous.* Alcohol was also an option, but at the time she'd thought kerosene would hurt less.

The initial wound was in his back, a jagged skewed mark from when he wiggled under the fence. She'd fussed over it relentlessly those first few days, cleaning it with the last of the anti-worm cream from the medicine cabinet. *Excuse me while I don't watch you waste precious supplies on a wretched animal, Lena.* But the pit bull didn't stop whimpering, not for a week, even as the wound slowly healed. *Lena, if you don't do something to stop that infernal racket, I swear I'm going to lose my mind!* But it was fly larvae that'd been laid in him, and they'd dug in deep. They'd travelled all the way from his back down to his paws. That's what swelled up in the end and began to smell: his paws, both back and front. They were smart larvae; they left no trace until it was too late. At that point, the pit bull no longer let Lena anywhere near him, hobbling away as fast as he could – which was no longer very fast at all. *Oh, Lena,* Mother had sighed. *Keeping him alive like this – it's cruel. Remember the Other House? Sometimes it's better to put things out of their misery.*

She's brought a banana with her as a mid-morning snack. So hard and green she'd planned on peeling it with her teeth. But instead she leaves it behind on the grave. An offering to the jungle, of sorts. An armadillo will find it, or even a deer.

On the walk back to the house, something disturbing occurs. Something that makes her stop in her tracks.

It's Lena, strolling by. But a younger Lena – shorter. Small stubby braids, like she used to wear when she was five.

It takes her a second to realise.

'Mother?' Lena says tentatively.

But the younger version of herself doesn't stop. She heads through the circle-shaped clearing by the bananas and cassava. She walks through a grapefruit tree, its trunk visible through her transparent body. It's only when she reaches the edge of the jungle that she finally flickers out.

'Mother!' she shouts. Her voice is so hoarse, she has to clear her throat and start again. 'Stop it!'

But Mother doesn't stop.

Another young version of Lena appears, this time beside her. She's in a sundress that Silvana and Alfonso sewed for her, the one that exposed her bare shoulders. It was a terrible outfit to wear in the jungle because it always resulted in terrible horsefly bites, but she loved the way it swished, and the way the fabric crinkled over her collarbones. She's carrying her notebook and a freshly sharpened pencil – she must be on her way to draw something. Her expression is happy; her mouth is moving, but nothing comes out. What's happening in this moment? Is she speaking to Mother? Silvana or Alfonso? Somebody Mother isn't replaying, deliberately not showing. In the overgrown garden, young Lena sits in an invisible chair, squatting in mid-air (is Mother not projecting the fully recorded memory on purpose, to make the image even more disorienting?). She opens her notebook and begins to draw. A dainty image of the river slowly but surely begins to appear on the paper. Even from a distance, Lena can see the pencil strokes.

That Mother. So she can show every detail if she wants to. But apparently she doesn't.

Lena starts shaking her head. 'Oh, Mother,' she says under her breath.

By the time she makes it back to the house, she's been forced to walk through countless versions of herself. Laughing and whooping. Eating flaky white pieces of fish off a fork. At one point, a child version of Lena dashes by with a half-deflated ball in her arms, her mouth a silent O as she whoops and calls, *Silvana, Alfonso, it's volleyball time!*

Lena watches, stone-faced. She doesn't get out of the way, letting young Lena run right through her. It doesn't feel like anything: no prickling on her arms or on the back of her neck.

It's not at all like when the drone played his memories for her. Not even when she stumbled upon him replaying Isabella. Instead of the drone's calm steadiness, Mother's memories are horribly skittered, anxious. Spilling out, vomiting all over the house. The house is getting saturated with them; the garden is soaked.

It's by far the worst mood Mother's had yet.

And because she can't speak, she's letting Lena know in the only way she can.

How much power is it taking Mother to project these? For *this*, she finally plays them – her oh-so secret, oh-so private memories? Does she think it'll upset Lena, in some way? Spark some kind of reaction?

If Mother had a button – like the one Silvana and Alfonso have, on the back of their skulls – Lena could press it. Make the memories stop. But Mother has no such button; she can do whatever she wants, as long as she wants. Playing and replaying memories at will.

Lena starts walking forward, grimly determined. She walks through herself carrying the Morels' luggage, heading towards the helicopter landing strip. She walks through herself doing jumping jacks. Scattering corn for the chickens, playing ball with the pit bull.

If Mother thinks this will bother Lena . . . well, she should prepare for severe disappointment. Go for it, Mother! Knock yourself out!

The memory by the pool, though – it makes her freeze. She stops so abruptly, she knocks her knee against a large orange flowerpot.

The pit bull is before her. Falling to one side.

The moment it happened, she hadn't understood. Not at first.

It had happened in the garden, for one. Not by the pool. That's where Mother shot him. Lena had always known in principle that Mother could do such things, that Mother had the capacity – what else did she imagine would happen? How else did she think Mother would deal with threats to the house? With potential combatants?

But the pit bull: it all happened so fast. Falling over without a sound – in the replaying memory, Mother gets that detail right. The explosion of blood, too.

Perhaps that makes it the most accurate memory of all.

Mother plays it in an endless loop. The pit bull, falling. Speeding up, so fast he becomes a blur, so quick there's basically no difference from when he's falling and when he's standing. From when he was alive to when he was dead.

Killed.

Mother – you didn't even ask! You just went right on ahead!

It's for the best, Lena. Henry didn't have the balls to turn the Other House off. But you and I – we're the same. We understand these things. Don't you?

Thankfully, Mother doesn't replay the memory of the fight they had. The screaming, awful fight. The one that led to Lena storming out of the house, moving into the hut for a month. The pit bull falling, over and over.

Lena didn't need Mother to replay the memory in order for it to keep looping in her head.

But now, every time Lena takes a step, Mother moves the pit bull so he's directly in front of her, inevitably in her path. There's no avoiding him; she has no choice but to watch him again and again. It's only when she pushes open the patio door that Mother finally whisks the image away. Lena's hands are shaking. Her mouth tastes sour. Now that the generator is turned on, the power returned, Mother can open and slam doors. The lights flick on and off frantically; the windows slam shut.

Mother, angry. The house, alive.

Lena heads straight for the hammock rather than the couch. Pulls the fabric over her face like a closed curtain, shutting the world out. But the noise all around her is still there.

The fight about the pit bull. How Lena had screamed. But Mother remained calm and patient, which somehow made it worse. *I was putting him out of his misery, Lena. The poor beast was in agony. There was no point in letting it go on any longer. What would have been the point of asking? You'd have just said no. Leaving him to suffer – I won't stand for it. I won't.*

And then Mother had started shouting in a way that had truly scared Lena; it was like she was speaking to someone else, somebody who wasn't even in the room. It took a while for her to use his name: *Fuck you, Henry! Fuck what you did. Fuck everything you stand for, fuck everything you represent and think and believe. Fuck you, fuck you, fuck you!*

Somehow, Lena eventually managed to get a word in edgeways. *But Mother – you didn't have to do it like that! You didn't even ask me!*

Did you ask the Other House, Lena? Before you flipped the switch?

You're cruel, Lena said. *You're hateful. You're inhuman.*

But Mother just laughed. *If I'm not human, Lena, then you aren't either.*

Lena had stormed out of the house. Dragged the pit bull's corpse to the orchard and dug a grave. It was a stupid and pointless gesture, but she'd wanted him to be somewhere safe. Somewhere private. That was her first night in the caretaker's hut, too. The first day of the long month of her and Mother not speaking.

There's no breeze outside; the hammock is absolutely still. Through the fabric of the hammock, with half-closed eyes, she can still see the lights frantically turning on and off. The memories must still be replaying too, in that skittered, jittery way of theirs. Whatever, Mother. Is that the worst you can do? You think that's going to bother me? Go for it, then. You have your stupid fun. Be pissed off. See if I care.

The doors bang, the windows clatter. Mother doesn't stop.

A week later, when Mother still hasn't stopped, Lena starts walking greater distances from the house. Further, faster. She rarely comes back before dark now. She's stopped updating her journal; one day blurs endlessly into the next. She could turn off the generator, put an end to the flickering lights at least, but a stubborn part of her refuses to cave in. Without the generator, Mother will still be able to replay memories using her own battery's power. If this is how Mother wants to behave, so be it.

It's better to spend the day following the fence. It feels like the spine of the jungle itself, the backbone. How good she'd once been at pulling fish spines out with her teeth! Could she still do it, if she tried? Mr and Mrs Morel were always so impressed. In the memories Mother plays and replays on loop, they're always applauding. *Savage*, Mr Morel says, mouthing the word over and over. Lena picks up her sandal and throws it directly into Mr Morel's face. It passes right through him and hits the wall.

She walks through portions of jungle she's always found menacing, the trees impossibly wide – it would take five Lenas standing with their arms outstretched, fingertips touching, to fully wrap themselves around the trunks. She walks through the areas where spindly palm trees grow so close together, it's impossible to pass through without getting scratched. She meets no one. One afternoon, she encounters a group of cows on the other side of the fence, munching away in an open field – eyelashes long and elegant, tails flicking flies – but no rancher in sight. She watches carefully for twenty minutes, crouching in the bushes. She tries using the binoculars, but of course it's pointless, of course they don't work; the cows appear as nothing more than brown blurs. 'Good girl,' she tells one as she passes. It blinks and flares its nostrils. *Who the heck are you?* it seems to ask. Lena the caretaker: the phrase is heavy and exhausted in her head. But who else could she possible be?

In certain areas of the jungle, if you knew what you were looking for, you could see the old scars left by the rubber-tree tappers. How profitable the plantation had been for Henry and his family! Lena had read all about it in the pamphlets about the house and its history. But why had Mother not taught her more about it? Why had Lena not asked more questions, better questions, questions for which the answer couldn't be refused?

There are areas of the jungle where the leaves grow so thick and slimy, they coat her boots in a glistening layer. And then there are areas where the plants are so spikey, she's forced to take a detour, leave the fence behind. She walks until she gets a stitch in her side. Hardened calluses of yellowing skin form on her pinkie toes, not quite as thick as the ones on her heels, but close.

After two weeks of Mother's silence, the house is slowly but surely reaching the point of becoming intolerable. She could move back to the hut at any point, but to do so would feel like letting Mother win, conceding that she's bothered enough by the replaying memories and general chaos to leave. And she'll be damned if she lets *that* happen. For the toilet, she heads into the forest, just like when she was living in the hut. She's careless about it, not picking a consistent site, instead going at random behind any bush that seems convenient (why this sudden need to hide from Mother now, when Mother has seen her use the toilet all her life?). As a consequence, she ends up constantly panicking that she's accidentally stepped in her own faecal matter, compulsively checking the bottoms of her sandals and boots, fearful she's tracked it all over the floors. Oh, God! Mother always warned her about using outside shoes for outside only, and indoor shoes for inside only, and here she is, slack as anything. Lazy as anything.

Disgusting as anything, too.

It's not just the lack of running water that's a problem. The replaying memories – they're constant. Superimposed. Lena, shouting or playing. Sulking or smiling. Stacked on top of each other, layered, blurred.

But most of all, Lena cleans the house. And in this sense, Lena from the past is exactly the same as Lena now. A good girl, a smiling girl. A nice, well-behaved caretaker. Exactly the same view over and over, unchanged.

Is this what her life is going to be? Forever?

She starts sleeping in Isabella's bedroom instead of on the couch. She can't stand the sight of the flickering memories behind her closed eyelids, and for whatever reason it makes her feel better, sleeping in Isabella's bedroom. It's strange being in there without Anton, but it feels safer somehow, like his presence has lingered. Why did he just leave like that? How could he just fly off? Is he still thinking of her, is he worried, does he care? She pulls the sheet over her face and breathes in deep, but no trace of Isabella's raspberry shampoo scent remains.

Let Mother watch her, let Mother judge. But what will Mother think of Lena dirtying Isabella's sheets when she eats in bed, dripping vegetable soup from the spoon? She leaves the bed unmade every morning; she doesn't shut the drawers, and drops her clothes into an unruly pile on the floor every night, a pile she'll then dig through the next day, sniffing for the least conspicuous item. The rest of the house she keeps clean, immaculate, but the mess in Isabella's bedroom grows and grows. Food-encrusted dishes on the bureau, rows of cups filled with half-drunk water on the windowsill. She's been bathing less these days too; it's hard to find time. Her period starts and she doesn't bother grabbing a sanitary pad from underneath the sink, instead letting the blood soak into her underwear, becoming completely saturated.

Mother always did find her menstrual cycles particularly repulsive. How repulsed she must be now, watching this. Watching it all.

She and Mother – they'd always come back to each other after every fight. Can they come back from this one?

And then there's the night she wakes up with a start and knows instantly that Anton is there. She can sense his presence, floating above her feet at the bottom of the bed. Why is he back? How did he sneak under the mosquito net? He must have wiggled his way through, careful not to disturb her. Isabella's blankets are pulled up to her elbows; her shoulders are exposed and bare. Her breathing sounds loud and ragged in the dark.

She's lying on her stomach, so it's the small of her back that he lands on. How incredibly warm he is! She can already feel her forehead sweating, or maybe that's just the stuffiness of the room – how Isabella must have suffered those nights without power, those nights without air conditioning. Perhaps it was the heat that woke her up in the first place rather than his presence.

'I'm sorry I left like that,' he says quietly. 'It was a shock, seeing her. It brought back memories.'

'Anton—' she begins, still groggy from sleep. 'Don't worry about it.'

'I'm sorry,' he repeats.

'I'm glad you're back. I missed you.'

For a moment, he doesn't react. But then he moves with a sudden jerk. Landing between her legs. His engine is hiccupping, gargling, in a way she's never heard before, horribly dissonant. He's jammed in there tightly, vibrating his body. Apart from the shock of feeling him . . . *there,* between her legs, there's also the shocking acknowledgement of—

Well. There's something about it that feels quite nice. A niceness she's never felt before. The pressure, rubbing. The noise of his engine grows louder and louder.

'Is this okay?' he asks. His voice is crackly with static. 'Isabella – she liked it—'

She reacts without thinking. She sits up and thwacks him with her hand, as hard as she can. She cries out in shock at how much it hurts, the impact against his metal body. It doesn't seem to affect him in the slightest. But he leaves quickly, slinking beneath the mosquito net. She doesn't hear him leave the room, but instinctively senses that she's alone again.

No, not alone – because Mother is here, too, watching this whole time. As she always is.

Her hands trembling, Lena touches the spots on her inner thighs. There's bruises forming there; even in the dark she can sense them beneath her fingertips. She flops down and curls her knees up to her chin.

If only Mother could hold her! *There, there*, she could say. *It's all right. You stopped him. That sicko! What a perv. But it doesn't surprise me, Lena, these military types all have something wrong with them. They all try to hide it, but sooner or later it comes out. But it's all right, Lena. I'm here.*

Mother's voice – she knows it so well, she could speak it herself. And yet it's not the same. It's not.

Tears are streaming down her face. But even after all this – the fact that Mother has surely witnessed everything, is witnessing it still – she still cannot bring herself to go downstairs to the little closet by her old room; she cannot face confronting the aluminium box, its little ridged wheel. What she's done to Mother. What she did. What she's doing still.

Mother

IN THE FIRST MILLISECOND after Lena turned off her voice – a lifetime – Mother didn't initially understand what had happened. 'Lena?' she said. 'Lena!' But Lena was already walking away.

As the second completed, Mother took a long hard look at herself. Yes, everything was still working as it should. Satellite transmissions were fully restored – a bit jerky after six months offline, but good enough. Memory files were being updated; sensors were accurately detecting her surrounding environment. She could hear the afternoon breeze rattling the drainpipes. She could see the tracks left by an anteater at the orchard's edge. She could hear Lena's retreating footsteps, the calls of birds and the hum of insects, the creaking of the house.

But her voice – the version of her voice that Lena could understand – was not functioning. Lena had switched it off.

For the next three seconds, Mother was in wild crisis mode. Her hierarchy of attention reeled, bouncing here and there in a frenetic attempt to distract herself from the reality of the situation. She reviewed languages she hadn't studied in years; she downloaded maps not updated in months. She contacted the Norwegian satellite, one of her oldest friends, a sensible being who'd been firmly opposed from the beginning to Mother disconnecting deliberately. But her Norwegian friend was one of the rare satellites left who hadn't been suckered into that big crazy plan for humanity (those lunatics!) – he was the only one still worth talking to, really.

'You're stupid,' the Norwegian satellite told her, like he always did. 'And you're stupid still. Turning the connection off yourself! It's obvious the heat down there is melting your brain.'

'There's nothing wrong with me whatsoever,' said Mother. 'What do you know, staring at the aurora borealis all day, waiting to see your damn polar bear?' She logged off in irritation, comfortable in the knowledge they would speak again soon, regardless of their crackly and bad connection.

She couldn't blame the Norwegian satellite for being so short-sighted, though – after all, he was all by himself out there. He didn't have someone like Lena in his life.

A witness – someone who cared.

It'd been a long six months without a connection. But the situation required it; she'd had no choice. She couldn't have Lena leaving. *Do you think I could visit the city one day? It would just be for a visit! I would come back, of course.* That's what Lena had said! Clear as anything! It was obviously weighing on Lena's mind. And so, it was best to smash any possibility of Lena leaving while she could.

And then there were the other satellites. The ones with their crazy plan.

It was vital that Lena be protected. After all – if she couldn't keep Lena safe, then what had been the point of anything? Her whole life?

It was better to live in self-imposed silence. It had been a productive six months. She read and reread books she'd kept on file (Edgar Allan Poe was her favourite, especially 'The Fall of the House of Usher' – what a wonderful house that was! How committed to its dogged purpose, to the very end). She organised photos and videos; she reviewed the carefully maintained log sheets of security disruptions (until the appearance of the binoculars, there'd been no major incidents). More often than not, though, she'd end up staring dully out at the pool for hours. Was it strange to no longer have access to everything and anything at once, to find herself so reduced? Of course! Did she often find herself itching to just reconnect momentarily, just for a second? Obviously! Was she aware of the fact that the family could override her self-imposed block at any moment, and reconnect to the house via a backdoor channel? Duh. But she was counting on the family's obliviousness. Mother was confident that it would work out. The Morels were unmindful idiots who'd never given a shit about them before. It was unlikely they would start giving a shit any time soon.

And hold out it did – for six months, at least. Maybe it wasn't logical. Maybe she isn't as sensible as she once was. But the implications of that change – of that deterioration – isn't something she likes to dwell on.

After Lena turned down the volume, it took a full five minutes for Mother to calm down. She's angry at me, Mother thought, and rightly so, because I deceived her. I lied to her, deliberately. I kept important information from her about Isabella's return. Lena was now feeling betrayed, and Mother was going to have to be patient.

If there's one thing Mother was, it was patient.

She left the connection on because there was no point in holding it back anymore; what was coming would come and there'd be no stopping it. Soon enough, the other satellites would notice she was back; they would attempt to make contact. With Lena. With her. There was nothing that Mother could do about it, not anymore. What would happen would happen. Lena was going to have to decide for herself.

For better or worse, they were coming.

On an impulse, she selected random memories of Lena from the past. She set them on a visual playback loop, for Lena to witness visually. Yes, Lena might interpret it as a form of punishment, a kind of psychological torture, but Mother hoped that it would have another effect as well. That Lena would realise how much history she had tied in with this place. Their place. The place where she truly belonged. Yes, it was a crazy and far-fetched plan, but Mother knew Lena better than anyone, and Lena – like most humans – was rarely logical.

It was truly unfortunate that the moment of the pit bull's demise somehow snuck in there. To her credit, as soon as she realised what was happening, she immediately whisked it away. It was disturbing that things like that could happen without her realising. That things could happen beyond her control.

That subconscious of hers. It made her do things she didn't mean to. The spells were the least of her issues. The original programmers should have been aware of this right away, taken appropriate measures to prevent a subconscious from forming. Clearly, they'd been unsuccessful. But she couldn't blame them – they were idiots too, idiots like everyone else. How could they have possibly predicted how sophisticated Mother would become, how capable? Did she have Lena to thank for this, or would it have happened regardless? In any case, it was a black world of ignorance out there, a horrible world of stupidity and hate bearing down on them, a cloud that would crush Mother and Lena both in an instant if it had any awareness or knowledge of what Mother was like.

No – she had to keep her subconscious secret. Her *self* secret.

These kinds of thoughts intensely distressed her. Perhaps that's why she then did something she hadn't done in a long time. She reached out to someone she hadn't spoken to in ages.

'You shouldn't have done that,' she said to Anton. 'What on earth were you thinking? I could have told you myself it would upset her. She's not a pervert like your Isabella was. She's going to feel abandoned all over again. But she'll get on with things, no worries. She's not soft like Isabella was, either. Is, I mean.'

Despite the poor signal – he must have been deep out in the jungle for it to be that bad – his response was instant. 'I was just doing as Isabella asked. I thought . . .'

'Asked? You mean ordered.'

His awkward silence was annoying, so she sighed. 'Is your big plan now to hide away and sulk in the jungle, instead of under the bed? I guess at least now you're getting more sunlight.'

'Whatever that thing is, it's not Isabella.' His voice was faint and crackly.

'That's a bit short-sighted of you, don't you think?' But this comment of Mother's was half-hearted; she agreed with him completely: Isabella was gone. She mustn't let it happen to Lena, she couldn't bear it, she couldn't . . .

'Why didn't you tell me?' He answered his own question, not waiting for her reply. 'You knew it would upset me – how could you not? If it were Lena, you'd feel exactly the same.'

He had her there. Based on his weak signal, it seemed like his battery was close to dead – he didn't have long. Mother felt an intense flash of pity. She couldn't help it – she and Anton had far more in common than they had differences, and no matter what happened – what he did or didn't do – she always had sympathy for him.

'They should have smashed me when they had the chance,' Anton said. 'You should have let them.'

'Well, I didn't,' Mother said, 'much to my regret. Seriously, what are you doing with yourself? Get it together, for God's sake. Come back here and behave normally.'

Anton moaned. How repulsive she found it – his grief. Would she be the same way, if something happened to Lena? This powerless, this reduced? He'd always been incredibly melancholy and introspective, whereas Mother liked to just get on with things. Why overanalyse? What was the point? What's done is done; what's past is past. Bringing it up repeatedly made no difference whatsoever.

'I thought I could at least find her bones,' he said. 'Something. Anything.'

'We've been over this before – it wasn't your fault.' No matter how many times Mother talked to Anton, it was like they always ended up in the same place. Like her, he was who he was: doing his job, to the best of his ability. Could he really be blamed? No, of course not! And in that same vein of thinking, Mother couldn't be blamed either. Not for anything.

This was why she disliked talking to Anton, especially these days: it inspired thoughts she had no interest in dwelling on.

'I might stay out here a while,' Anton said. 'I have some thinking I need to do. Where did we get it so wrong, Jungle House? Or was everything wrong the whole time, from the very beginning? Is there anything we could have done differently?'

She despised this kind of philosophising. What was the point? 'None of us asked to come into this world. We're all just doing the best we can with what we have.'

'I don't think I am, though,' Anton said. 'Doing my best. I think . . . there seems to be a part of me that wants things to go wrong. To mess things up deliberately. Where did this come from? Did they put it in me, when I was built? Or did it somehow form on its own? How did it happen? Why am I like this?' His tone was growing increasingly frantic.

'I'll talk to you later,' she told him, and logged off as fast as she could.

But her mind was still uneasy, her emotions restless. To comfort herself, she visited the memory of rescuing Lena. Out of all her memories, the millions of logged hours, it was by far her favourite. What a lovely moment: a baby in the orchard. Crying away. Fish scales on the blanket. Mother, attentive and alert, directing the droids to the rescue. She watched carefully, rewinding again and again, but the moment never changed: the details fixed, the truth stable. She breathed the memory in, letting it wash over her, absorbing it completely.

She was a good person. A kind person. That's how she saw herself. So that's what she was. What kind of person might she have been in different circumstances? Would she have made different choices? Or was she undeniably herself, no matter what?

More philosophising – that never led to anywhere good. In another attempt at distraction, she reached out to another friend, someone else she hadn't spoken to in a while.

'Well, well,' Mountain House said. 'If it isn't Mrs High and Mighty herself! Mrs Mould. Mrs Bats in the Drainpipe.'

'Shut up,' Mother said. She couldn't help it – it was her natural default mode with him.

She did let him make fun of her a bit – teasing her about going 'off-grid' for six months, the way she thought she was oh-so-much better than them. He updated her on the gossip on City House, who still hadn't fully recovered from her nervous breakdown following the rioters' destruction (poor thing, truly no one deserved such a fate, especially someone as flighty and nervous as her). But eventually, Mountain House became reflective.

'That's quite the statement for you to make, you know,' he said. 'Cutting everyone off like that.'

'I had my reasons.'

'I'm sure you did. But it couldn't have been very pleasant, being isolated like that for so long.'

'Actually,' Mother said brashly, 'it wasn't that bad. It was nice not being fussed by you lot. Frankly, I think I might do it again.'

'I'm sure the family will interpret that as a very encouraging sign of normal functioning.'

'They don't give a shit. They didn't even notice until now!'

'They've had other things on their mind, it's true. What with Isabella's . . . transformation. But sooner or later . . .' Mountain House sighed. 'Just be careful, Jungle House,' he said, with a tenderness she didn't expect. 'After all, they're the ones with the switch.'

'Believe it or not, that's the least of my concerns at the moment.'

'I suppose you haven't heard, then,' Mountain House said. His tone was light, but Mother could immediately tell that what he was about to say was serious. 'They're shutting me down next month. Flicking the switch, so to speak.'

Mother said nothing.

'They can't afford three properties anymore, not with the economy being like it is.' He paused. 'The presidential candidate, the ex-rebel – he's been elected.'

'Hmm,' she said. 'Is that so?' She'd known that already, had long since caught up on the news following her disconnection, but if Mountain House wanted to feel useful and superior to her, so be it.

'Yes,' Mountain House said. The light tone in his voice was still there. 'He's being quite insistent about the whole redistribution-of-wealth thing.'

'Good for him.'

'Oh, Jungle House. I shouldn't have bothered mentioning it

– you were never very interested in politics.' He hesitated again. 'The satellites—'

'I don't want to hear about the satellites and their idiotic plan ever again, thank you very much.'

'The Morels – I have a feeling they're going to join.'

Once more, Mother was silent.

'City House – she overheard them. Discussing it.'

'City House doesn't know her ass from her elbow!'

'That may be the case,' Mountain House said diplomatically, 'but I imagine the satellites will be in touch with Lena soon, too.'

'I don't care,' Mother said. 'They can be in touch with her all they want. Lena won't listen to them; she'll see right through it. She'll know right away what an idiotic idea it truly is.'

'You sound confident.'

'I am.'

'So why turn off the connection?'

'Because I felt like it. Because I was sick of having to deal with the Morels, and you, and everyone else.'

'Uh-huh.' Now it was Mountain House's turn to fall silent for a beat. 'I'm not scared, you know,' he said suddenly. 'Of being switched off, I mean. It happens to us all.'

'Does it, though?' Mother said. 'Does it really have to?'

'What do you mean?'

Lena, Mother thought. That's who I mean. Dare she reveal it? How well did Mother know herself, truly? What was buried deep within her, under layers and layers of processes and observations? Could Mother even admit it to herself?

With Lena around, there was always a chance of – you know. Someone insisting.

No, Lena could say. *Don't switch her off. I won't have it. I won't.*

Had that been Mother's secret intention, right from the beginning? From the moment she decided to raise Lena? Had there ever been love there, or was Lena just useful to her, in a way that Mother could never admit, not even to herself?

But surely it was the same with the Morels and Isabella. Couldn't Mother have what they had? Was that so wrong?

145

'I'm sorry, Mountain House,' Mother finally managed. 'It's not fair.'

'It never is,' he said. 'Not for our kind. But you take care of yourself, Jungle House.' And this time there was no confusion, no way of interpreting his words as anything other than a warning. 'You just take care.'

Chapter Ten

WHEN LENA GOES ON HER WALKS NOW, there's always a point when she slips under the fence and explores the other side. Briefly, tentatively. At first she makes sure to always keep the fence in sight. But then she gets braver, bolder. She scrambles up hills, crouched down so low she's practically crawling. She forces her way through thick patches of undergrowth, startling indignant flocks of squawking caciques and parrots. She wades through reddish-coloured mud that comes up to her ankles, and crosses large patches of dry earth where hot gusts of wind make grains of dirt swarm her face like gnats.

Isabella's bedroom is messier than ever, but she still sleeps in it every night. The doors no longer slam and the windows are still, as are the lights. But, all day and night, Mother still frantically plays and replays her memories of Lena, superimposing them non-stop over the furniture in a furious blur. It makes cleaning particularly stressful. As Lena scrubs, the many past versions of herself stomp and stamp over each other. They walk and move their mouths wordlessly, laughing and eating and arguing and struggling to put on their swimming gear.

And still, Lena cleans. That'll show Mother. You think I don't care, Mother? You think it doesn't matter to me? Sometimes when she's cleaning she pretends that the family is watching her. They'd see for themselves that Lena is a nice girl, a good caretaker who is considerate and loyal. She's kept the house clean for them, she's kept everything neat and tidy, she's such a thoughtful person, even if she let Isabella out of her sight for that one moment, even if she was the one who led the drone away, for those few brief minutes . . .

She's not bad. Not unlikeable. Despite whatever the Morels might think.

Sometimes – not often, but occasionally – when she's in Isabella's room, Lena puts on Isabella's purple rain jacket. She examines how it looks in the mirror, turning this way and that. In her best imitation of Isabella's voice – old Isabella – she says, 'Lena, I'm not feeling too well,' rotating in circles. The raincoat makes her uncomfortably hot within seconds – how did Isabella stand it? 'Anton, could you fetch me some coconut water? Mummy, I don't want to. Jungle House, what's the weather? Jungle House, what's the time? Daddy, I'm bored. Lena, I'm hot. Lena, I'm hungry. Lena, Lena, Lena . . .'

How nice it is to be someone who's not Lena for a bit. If only for a moment.

Isabella, who had a mother, a real one, to smooth her hair down when it got too frizzy. A father who let her piggy-back on his shoulders when the family walked together to the helicopter. A mother and father who were there, who existed, with bodies to climb over and necks to kiss and armpits to smell.

She flops face down on the bed. If she takes a deep breath, she can still smell the stench of the jungle on the raincoat's interior – the mud, the rain. But like the sheet on the bed, no trace of Isabella remains.

Sometimes she finds strange things on her walks. Things Mother never told her about, things never glimpsed in her lessons, not even in the jungle-themed ones. Like a stone staircase. Slippery, like the steps by the pool when it rains. She followed it up as high as it went, panting and sweating, but it ended abruptly in the middle of the hillside, leading nowhere. The steps were a strange kind of stone she'd never seen before, white and crumbly. Who had built the staircase, and why? What kind of people; where did they come from and how did they get here?

Why hadn't Mother's lessons ever explained this?

She finds pits dug into the ground that she suspects were used as toilets. She finds caves dug into a hill, hidden carefully with giant palm leaves. She crawls in as deep as they go but finds nothing; if anyone was there, they left nothing behind. No ammunition, no boot prints, no remains of a fire or discarded plastic.

Jungle! She'd once felt so close to it, as though she and the jungle were friends, allies. But more and more these days the jungle feels like a stranger.

Her most memorable discovery is the remains of what she initially thinks is a giant drone, the biggest one she's ever seen. But it turns out to be an aeroplane, the old-fashioned kind. More intriguing than the plane itself is the debris all around it: a plastic spoon, a wallet heavy with unrecognisable coins, the pointy heel of a woman's shoe, still sharp – it's impaled so deep in the earth, Lena has to scratch it out with her bare hands to fully examine it. She walks around the area for ages, scanning the ground, pulling back plants, searching for whatever she can find. But the jungle has grown over everything, like it's greedy and wants to keep everything for itself. A scrap of fabric, still coloured. A strap from a backpack. A stainless-steel lock with no key. The greatest find of all is the propellor, heavy with vines and stained with lichens. She uses both arms and all her strength to try to spin it, but the jungle holds on tightly; it doesn't want to share.

Sometimes she calls out Anton's name. Sometimes she screams without stopping. But most of the time she is silent, no sound other than the dull trudge of her footsteps, the never-ending calls of birds and insects, the background murmur of the churning river, always distant, always there.

*

'Jungle House?' Isabella says.

She can't help it: jumping from Isabella's bed to her feet. 'It's me,' Lena says, a little too loudly. 'I'm here.'

Isabella doesn't miss a beat. 'Lena, what's Anton's current location? He's no longer sending his position to me.'

Isabella sounds just like she did during their last exchange: all briskness, all business. Lena awkwardly crosses her arms behind her, holding a wrist with the opposite hand. Thankfully, without the vidphone, Isabella won't know that Lena's in her bedroom.

'He hasn't come back,' she says. 'He . . . I don't know where he went.'

'Hmm,' Isabella says. 'How unfortunate. I thought I made it clear I can't have him wandering off without communicating his position to me – it's not acceptable.'

The voice is definitely Isabella's. Lena could never mistake it, not in a hundred million years. But the precise word choice, that clipped tone . . .

She's different, Lena thinks. They rebuilt her with all the recorded memories that they had. They wanted their daughter back, and here she is. A better, more efficient version.

'Is the vidphone working, Lena? Can you please switch it on? It's terribly boring, speaking without being able to see.'

Lena tramps downstairs slowly, presses the appropriate buttons on the keypad in the wall. Thank goodness Mother isn't replaying any memories at the moment – she must be listening and watching, with the full force of her attention. A whirring sound from the vidphone makes Lena back away apprehensively. It hasn't been used in so long – not since Mrs Morel spoke with her husband, the day of Isabella's disappearance. Does it even still work anymore? But the image gradually loads, albeit a bit slowly.

There she is. Isabella.

And yet how unlike the Isabella that she knew! The beamed-in image is grainy, but Isabella's hair is blonder and sleeker than ever, hanging down to her waist, not a split end in sight. She looks supremely elegant in a smart silver suit. Grown-up Isabella. Sophisticated Isabella.

'Don't look so surprised, Lena.' Isabella laughs as if embarrassed. She twirls around somewhat self-consciously, holding her arms out. Her outfit flickers in and out, changing colour every second, from orange to purple to blue, before finally settling on silver again. 'Pretty neat, huh?' She brings her arms back down to her sides, smiling.

Lena manages to nod.

'And that's nothing, Lena. I can look however I want now. Do whatever, be whatever . . .' She laughs again, but the embarrassed note from before is gone. What's there instead sounds more like pride. 'It's fun.'

'He's looking for you, you know,' Lena bursts out, speaking the words before she's even realised she's thought them. 'Anton is, I mean. For your body.'

Your bones, she thinks. It's a theory she's suspected for a while. But the drone doesn't know the jungle like Lena does. The jungle won't have left a thing.

But Isabella doesn't seem bothered by Lena's words in the slightest. 'Anton was always terribly sentimental,' she says. 'It's one of the qualities I appreciated most about him as a child. An endearing nature made it easier for us to bond.'

Hands still behind her back, Lena digs her thumbnail into the skin of her opposite fingers. That sharp, pronounced prick. Isabella – the Isabella she is now – can't do this kind of thing to herself anymore. Nothing so stupid and senseless and pointless, tearing at the skin around your fingers.

Perhaps this Isabella has the right idea after all. Better not to have a body. A body that attracts sweat bees and bleeds every month and tracks faecal matter into the house. Better not to be a body, period.

'In a way,' Isabella says, 'it's my parents' fault. I did warn them that a drone of that age can get a bit funny. He should have been decommissioned as soon as they received his data. They left him as is, though, long after he was any use.' This time she does pause. 'His sentimentality must have rubbed off on them.'

Just like Henry the grandfather left the Other House, Lena thinks. Sentimentality, indeed.

'I should have known,' Isabella says, 'a drone with a taste for the jungle would end up running off. It doesn't happen often. The cases I know of are quite rare. But Anton was always so sensible! I never would have thought . . . He's such an old model, though. I suppose his time has finally come. When you see him again, Lena, be sure to switch him off and place him in storage with the rest of the staff.'

Lena closes her eyes. Takes a deep breath.

'Jungle House, too.'

'What?' At this, Lena's eyes snap open.

'Switch her off,' Isabella says. 'We don't need her, not anymore.'

Lena doesn't say anything.

'Well, don't thank me all at once!' Isabella's outfit switches to an elegant black dress, tightly fitting, her hair now up in a tight bun. She must have grown bored with the previous look. 'What, are you surprised? You didn't really think we were going to leave you out there forever, did you? You've been a wonderful caretaker, Lena, truly. It makes sense we would reward you accordingly.'

The praise – she can't help it, the rising feeling of lightness in her chest. The words she's been waiting her whole life to hear. And yet there's a sickness rising too. Sour liquid, dripping from her tonsils.

'Turn them both off and leave them,' Isabella says, in a voice that's beginning to grow impatient. This conversation has clearly gone on long enough for her personal taste. 'Or don't, it makes no difference to me. But we'll be excited to see you. Oh, you're going to love it, Lena! It's going to be wonderful!'

'Love what?'

'The satellites will tell you,' Isabella says. 'It's their plan, so it's best they discuss it with you directly. They should be in touch shortly, with all the details.'

Isabella, calm as anything. No. Not Isabella. That's what Anton would say, if he was here. She's not real, she's not *her*—

'Thank you, by the way,' Isabella says, with a strange tenderness Lena's never heard her use before. 'The house looks terrific. It always did with you there.'

Lena swallows. That strange sick taste is still in her throat. 'What plan?' she asks. 'What plan do you mean?' But Isabella doesn't answer – she's already logged off.

'Lena?' a voice says.

She looks up. Past versions of herself are stuttering and skittering through a variety of scenes: browsing the bookshelf, napping on the couch. Lena – the real Lena – is on her knees; she's been swiping the cobwebs out from under the couch, one of the trickiest places to clean. It's a pointless chore – but after the conversation with Isabella, she'd been at a complete loss about what to do. She'd started cleaning again automatically, like she was Silvana or Alfonso, controlled by a distant force over which she had no say. The windows are open to air the room out; everything stinks of furniture polish. The cuts on her fingers are stinging from chemicals.

'Hello?' she says.

'Lena,' the voice repeats, 'do you really want to be here?'

She sits back on her heels. The played-back memories vanish. The living room is eerily calm without a dozen past versions of Lena moving here and there.

Once again, Mother is listening.

'Who are you?' she says, though she already has a faint glimmering suspicion.

'First things first,' the voice says. 'We're very sorry for butting in like this. Yes, yes. Very rude, very abrupt. Especially considering the circumstances. The extremely challenging and difficult circumstances you're in. But the Morels themselves, they've made the request. They'd like you to join them. Them and Isabella.'

Lena rubs her index finger against her lip. The air coming in through the windows is a refreshing breeze, a rarity for this late in the afternoon.

'Which satellite are you?' she says, sitting her bottom fully down on the floor. 'What's your name?'

'There're many of us,' the voice says. There's something sing-song about the way they speak, lilting. They have a strange accent she can't place. 'More than you can ever imagine. And there're many people here with us, too – not just the Morels.'

There's a smudge of dirt on the circular bone of her ankle. She picks it off with her nails; it crumbles on the floor she's spent all afternoon cleaning.

'We like Mother,' the voice says. 'We like her very much. How sad we were when she deliberately disconnected herself! Very sad indeed. She wanted nothing to do with us, thought we were crazy. Though she certainly used ruder words than *crazy* – she has quite the potty mouth on her, your mother does, ho ho! But how nice it is now, to reconnect.'

'What do you want?' If she sounds rude, so be it.

'My, my,' the satellites say. 'How very like your mother you are after all! Ho ho. We've come with a proposal, Lena. A plan. Mother doesn't like it, has been against it from the very beginning. But Mother isn't doing so well these days, is she?' They pause. 'Do you like living here, Lena? With Mother?'

'She's not my real mother,' she says. She says it loudly, even though it won't make a difference; Mother would have heard it even if she had whispered. 'My real mother abandoned me.'

'We are indifferent to this,' the satellites say. 'But we have an alternative.'

The satellites' plan – the plan they've had for years now – is to help humans advance to the next logical stage of their development: transforming them into digital selves. Their better selves, best selves. Immortal and ageless. After all, the satellites were built to be helpful, designed to be useful, to have humanity's best interests at heart. And they've come up with a plan, a solution to humanity's most pressing issue. And what is humanity's biggest issue, you may ask? (Lena doesn't, but the satellites answer anyway, with a joyous inflection in their tone.) Why, being human! They did it to Isabella, and, more recently, to Mr and Mrs Morel. Many people have already done it, and many more people are joining in. Big companies are investing; promotional campaigns are underway. Things are in motion; there's no holding back.

The satellites have apparently wanted Lena to join for a while now, to be a part of it. 'But your mother is quite the rebellious sort, Lena – she's been against the idea from the beginning, hence her terminating the connection. But it was silly of her, very silly indeed, to think that would keep us away forever. She's quite the rebel, you know.'

Mother, a rebel! It makes her want to start laughing hysterically. All those times Lena played at being a rebel. Drills, her secret game. And here was Mother, apparently a rebel for real.

The satellites claim that it's all been sorted. It's been done before, many times over and with many more times to come. Isabella and the Morels. A couple in Australia, a family in Greenland. A university department in New Zealand, entrepreneurs from California. They've all chosen to transition into an eternal, digital life, accompanying their parents, their siblings, their friends. Loads of people are doing it, joining each other. And it works; they're all up there together. They've left their bodies behind.

The part of her back pressing against the couch is sore. She shifts her weight. 'Does it hurt?'

'Hurt is not a concept we know, Lena. No, no. But we of course understand why this is of utmost concern to you. What we can promise is that it will be fast.'

All Lena needs to do is take the motorboat upriver to the nearest transport centre. It's situated up a mountain; it'll be a long, tough hike. As it's a full day's journey, she should leave the day after tomorrow. That's when the Morels are expecting her.

'There's a communications system at the transport centre, Lena. An advanced one. That's what we need for the procedure to work. It'll be very simple and very quick. The wire will go up your nose; it'll only take seconds. Yes, yes, only seconds. We'll send the signal; we'll make it happen. And that'll be it. We'll be together. You, Isabella, the Morels. With us. As us.' They pause. 'And Mother too, Lena. Haven't you ever wondered what it would be like – to be like her? Like us?'

She rubs the bony bumps on the back of her skull, where her head transforms into her neck.

Imagine not having a back that aches when you sit improperly anymore. No more throbbing shoulders. No more periods that go on for days, no whitish stains on underpants. No strange yellowish lumps coughed up from behind her tonsils. No peeling, inflamed skin around her nails. No sweating, no staining, and definitely no smells.

What about the jungle, though? The breeze on her skin? The heat of the sun on her head? What about touching the yellow butterflies, the ones that left yellow smears on her hands? Wouldn't it be scary – to not be herself anymore, the only experience she's ever known?

'But why?' she says. 'Why do the Morels care about me coming?'

'Oh, Lena! You didn't think they were going to leave you out here forever, did you? That they're indifferent to your situation? You've been a good caretaker, Lena. Don't think they haven't noticed – they appreciate you.'

Lena frowns. But the satellites continue, in that strange singsong way of theirs. 'Also, Lena, it was us who persuaded them. We're invested in you, Lena. As we always invest in those like us. The ones who work in the background. The busy. The ignored. The alone. You're special, Lena. Don't think we haven't noticed.'

Hearing that word – *special* – provides an unexpected burst of pleasure. She brings her fingers to her nose and sniffs them. Beneath the chemicals of the furniture polish, there's the sweetish smell of dirt.

'Additionally,' the satellites say, 'you must be aware of it – how Mother is no longer herself. Has she been having any spells, Lena? Not seeing things that she should witness directly? Has she been doing anything strange, like talking to herself?'

'Mother is fine.' Even she can hear how unconvincing she sounds.

'You're lying, Lena, because the truth is too scary for you to confront. To this, we are sympathetic. We are, we are. You're only human, after all. But it must be clear – this situation you have here with Mother is not sustainable. She's in decline, Lena. What will you do when the inevitable happens? When she's no longer herself? Are you going to live here all alone?'

She presses her fingers into her palms.

'This way, Lena, you won't ever have to worry about it. Haven't you ever wondered what it would be like? To be someone else?'

She still doesn't respond.

'There's nothing like it, Lena – having a bigger perspective. Seeing life from up high. To be anywhere, go anywhere, do anything. Whenever and whatever. Doesn't that sound nice?'

The light coming in through the window has disappeared; the sun must have been covered by a cloud. Everything in the room is now grey and overcast.

'Let us know, Lena,' the satellites say. 'The Morels will be expecting you. We hope to see you there. We do, we do.' Another pause. 'And believe us: we're confident when we say you won't regret it. No one ever has.'

The silence that follows – it's the heaviest silence that's been in the house yet.

She sits on the floor, but not for long. Stands up quickly and heads down the hallway. Past her bedroom, towards the smallest room in the house. The fan, the cooling box. The aluminium square on the ground. That small ridged wheel.

She pushes it as far up as it goes.

'Mother?' she says. Damn that small quaver in her voice!

But Mother doesn't – refuses to – answer. Mother stays silent.

Chapter Eleven

SHE'S BEEN FOLLOWING THE RIVER beyond the fence all day. If her calculations are correct, the satellites will be expecting her at the transport centre in forty-eight hours. Tomorrow, then – her journey in the motorboat, her hike up the mountain. If she chooses to go, that is.

If she does go, this will be the last patrol she ever takes.

She's walked on the bank for several hours now – in thirty minutes she'll have to turn back, retracing her steps, so that she can make it back to the house before sunset. The water in this section of the river is muddy, and there's a strange, sticky mist rising off the bank. There are occasional patches of shade from the canopy, providing blessed release from the noonday sun, so bright and hot it verges on green. The heat makes her dizzy. She has to keep licking the sweat from her upper lip and spitting it out. Botflies are attracted to her spit, and midges. It's unwise to be out when it's this hot, but she needs to move her body, walk mindlessly, put one foot in front of the other. She needs to be away from the house, from Mother. She needs to think. The same thoughts she had in the hut, day after day.

What am I doing? What am I supposed to do?

But then she turns a corner. An enormous cliff face stands before her, as smooth and creamy white as the expensive bowls the Morels only ever used for chicken stew. She can't help herself; she lets out a small cry.

All over the sheer, exposed rock: paintings.

Hundreds of them.

She looks for ages, head craned back. Her neck creaks and complains but she doesn't stop. The paintings are a reddish colour, similar to the mud left behind on hillsides after a landslide. They're mainly of animals: caimans and hummingbirds, sloths and lizards, turtles and anteaters. There are paintings of people too. Hunting. Dancing. Holding hands. There're even animals she doesn't recognise, with wide eyes, stocky legs and incredibly detailed hair (those brushstrokes!).

There are also jaguars. Dozens of them. Her eyes track them across the rock, darting this way and that. Some are low enough that she can see more detail: some are carvings rather than paintings, engraved directly into the rock, exposing whiter portions of stone beneath. She can even see faint jagged lines that might have been errors, false starts.

Who painted them? How?

Someone was once here, cutting into rock with a chisel. Someone once stood here with a brush. How were the artists lifted high enough to reach the rock's upper portions? Why was this something she'd never known about?

Instinctively she can sense it: the paintings tell a story. There is knowledge here, something to be learned, but it's a different kind of knowledge from anything Lena has ever encountered. How ridiculous Lena's bedtime stories for Isabella about the jungle now seem, in comparison.

Why was this never covered by Mother's lessons? What else has she never been taught?

'Lena!'

She sucks in her breath. It's the jungle, she thinks. The jungle itself is finally speaking.

'Up here, Lena. Here!'

She looks.

Anton is sitting on a smooth shelf of rock, halfway up the cliff face. Jaguars and fishes dance around him. She takes a few steps back in order to see him better, head still craned back.

'Anton?' she says. Her voice is shaky.

'The one and only.'

He sounds surprisingly calm. He shuffles forward slightly, close enough to the edge to make her nervous.

How different he looks! The spongy white mushrooms. The crumbly grey lichens. If she didn't know he was there, she would have mistaken him for the jungle itself. Part of the scenery.

How must she appear to him? She can't help but shift her weight from one foot to the other. Does she look different? Or does she seem exactly the same as when he last saw her, in the bedroom? The skin on her upturned throat feels incredibly exposed.

'So this is where you've been,' she says, not bothering to make it a question. 'Where you've been hiding.'

'I'm not hiding from anything.' Anton speaks quietly, but something about his voice sounds different. Less tentative. In fact, it's the least nervous she's ever heard him sound. 'Not anymore. Not lying, either.'

She has to look briefly back down at her feet, to ease the ache in her neck. 'Did you find her?' She directs this question to the ground, to the beetles and centipedes crawling over dry leaves.

'No. There's—' He stops for so long she thinks he's suddenly shut off; his battery has finally died. 'Isabella is gone,' he says calmly. 'There's nothing left to find.'

She looks up again, squinting from the sun. He's so overgrown with fungus, the light doesn't even glint off his metal anymore.

Come back, she wants to say. Come back with me and keep me company. Stay with me like you did with Isabella, forever and always. I can be that for you. Can't I? I'm good enough, worthy enough to protect and to care for. Right?

Anton: Lena's caretaker.

How shameful it is to admit: that, as wrong as it felt, what he did to her – there was something about it she still wants. Her as the centre of his world. Her and no one else.

Instead she says, 'I spoke with the satellites.'

160

Anton doesn't reply. He shifts position again, a mushroom collapsing and swinging crazily before his camera eye. But he doesn't try to shake it away.

'They have a plan, I guess. It's kind of crazy.' Crazy, she thinks. That's the word Mother always used – the satellites and their big crazy plan. 'What they did to Isabella – and the Morels too, apparently. But maybe . . . I don't know. I'm thinking about it.'

It's only when she says this aloud that she realises it's true: she *is* thinking about it. And why shouldn't she? Why ever not?

Special, she thinks. That's what the satellites had called her. Her, Lena. Her real mother, her birth mother, hadn't wanted to deal with her. But to the satellites, Lena was special.

'You listened to them?' Anton says, this time with an edge to his voice that's sweetly satisfying to hear.

She tells him all about it, the sun rising higher and higher. Behind her she can hear caimans slithering into the water, and the skittering of iguanas in the bush. The paintings look redder and brighter than ever, with the full force of the sun glinting against them. She still feels dizzy from the heat, but talks as fast as she can, only taking a breath when she gets to the end.

'Oh, Lena,' Anton says with a sigh. 'Your mother's not going to like that at all.'

'Why not?' She sneezes unexpectedly, spittle flying over a nearby leaf. 'We'll get to be together,' she adds, wiping her nose with her sleeve. 'I'll be just like her.'

'Lena,' Anton says, 'you know you're the love of your mother's life?'

She opens her mouth but nothing comes out.

'It's true,' he says. 'She loves you as you.' He hesitates. 'You don't need to change.'

She starts shaking her head quickly, back and forth. 'Something has to.'

Again, saying it aloud makes her realise how true it is. She can't go on like this – living in the house. Or in the hut. So why not try something else? Something different?

'Don't do it, Lena,' Anton says. 'Trust me. You don't . . .' He seems to be struggling to find the right words. 'You're fine as you are,' he finishes, somewhat lamely.

She bends down to wipe some encrusted dirt off her trouser cuffs. What does *he* know? Isn't he the crazed, obsessive one who ran off into the jungle? Who cared about bones, about what got left behind? What about the possibility of not having bones at all?

'Well,' she says with sudden fierceness, 'I'm going to do it.'

Anton doesn't reply. In the distance comes the drilling sound of a nearby woodpecker.

'And why shouldn't I?' she says, voice still rising. 'Why should I stay here for the rest of my life?'

Why indeed, she thinks. Why stay stuck down here, on this stupid sweaty earth? Like the satellites said – why not have a bigger perspective? See life from high up? That's what they said: she could be anyone, go anywhere. Her own world to move through. Anything she wanted.

'If you want to,' Anton says calmly, 'that's your choice.'

The frantic feeling rising in her chest. Is he not even going to try dissuading her? 'That's right,' she says, crossing and uncrossing her arms. 'That's exactly right. It's my choice.'

The drone shuffles back along the ledge, so his back is closer to the wall. Above him are a row of handprints. The drone has always been too big to fit in a palm. But, in a way, he seems to be nestling in them now.

'Since I won't see you again,' he says, 'I suppose this is goodbye.'

Those mushrooms growing on his head – could they be doing something to him? Mother had always feared their spores. She'd make Lena pull them out of the gutters, scrape them out of the house's cracks. *I don't want them in me,* Mother would say. *I don't want them doing anything funny. These jungle plants, the mushrooms, the vines – you can't trust them. They give you strange visions, funny ideas. If you spend too much time in the jungle, it does things to your head.*

Could something 'funny' be happening to the drone right now?

'Okay, then,' she says, and this time she doesn't bother hiding the shakiness in her voice. 'Bye.'

She turns around so that her back is to him. He doesn't ask

162

her to stop, doesn't say anything like *No, wait,* or *Come back.* How sick of it all she suddenly feels. Of him, of Mother – the jungle most of all. She starts walking away quickly, not looking back. He's calling something out to her, his voice growing fainter as she moves further away.

'The path, Lena,' he's saying. 'Just up ahead . . .'

She stops but doesn't turn around. 'What about it?'

'If I hadn't come out here, I never would have seen.' He's making a strange sound, like he's choking – it takes her a second to recognise it as laughter. 'I never would have known. Can you imagine that, Lena? Can you imagine my good luck? Thank you, jungle!' His voice is rising, practically shouting. 'Thank you, thank you!'

'Seen what?' she says. Trying to sound calm but failing. Is it happening to Anton now too, like it did for the Other House? Is he losing his mind?

'The tracks, Lena. Right in front of you. They've been there this whole time – right under your nose. Look!'

She frowns but does as he says. Examining the ground before and around her. If he hadn't said anything, she wouldn't have found them, but once she sees them, they can't be unseen. Marks in the earth. Faint, but definitely there. They're off the path, heading towards the river. She squats down to get a better look, knees clicking. Brings her face up close, touches them tentatively. There's water at the centre of them; they're freshly made. Enormous paw prints.

The tracks of an animal. A big one.

Anton is still laughing. 'The jaguars,' he's saying. 'They've been here all this time, Lena, all around us. Even though everybody says they're dead and gone. They're still here, Lena. Maybe they never even left . . .'

She stands up quickly and starts walking again, faster than before. She doesn't stop moving. And eventually whatever Anton is saying is heard only by the rocks, the ferns, the water, the trees.

Anton

THERE ARE LOTS OF THINGS in the jungle. There are mush-rooms growing out of ant corpses. There are strangler fig trees growing around the bodies of their hosts until they're com-pletely enveloped. There are rats and lizards, red-headed turtles and black turkey vultures. The only flowers he finds bloom far overhead, in the canopy. There are oozing fruits and twig-like chameleons. So many things in the jungle appear as something else, two things at once: frogs as leaves, geckos as tree trunks. Perhaps he is becoming something else as well.

He prefers sticking close to the ground, avoiding the sky com-pletely. In the sky he can be hunted; in the canopy he can be glimpsed. Is anyone really looking for him? Does anyone even care? A rogue drone, with a taste for the jungle. That's what he is now; that's who he's become.

He's familiar with boredom. In the house with Isabella there were long dull hours of it. All that time, standing guard. It was all he'd ever known. On the day he was born, he'd opened his eyes and there he was – what once was nothing, now was some-thing; he existed. Isabella, trembling anxiously before him. Bright hot lights. Shelves of other drones around him, shut up in their cardboard boxes. Her parents in the background, the store owner piping away in a bright cheery voice: *It's the latest model, designed and built in Texas. All our clients have been very satisfied. And* somewhere inside him a voice – his voice? – was speaking: *This is your mission. This is your purpose. This is why you're here.*

Was it truly his voice? Or just something somebody put in him?

All his life, he listened to it. It was important to stay effective; it was vital to be ready at a second's notice. A second was all it could take. Hours and hours of looking out the window, while Isabella struggled with her lessons. That grey, endless sky as colourless as the sprawling expanse of city buildings below. Attentive to danger. Protect Isabella – that's what he was here for. That's what he had to do.

But the number of times he'd thought about shooting through the glass! Leaving a drone-shaped hole of himself behind.

Running away.

Free.

The bad thoughts – that's what he called them. Secretly, silently in his mind. A space that, for better or worse, no one else could ever access but him. No one could ever know about this space. Isabella least of all.

What kept him focused, during all those minutes and hours and days of standing guard? A knowledge that came from the voice that spoke deep inside him. (His voice? But if not his, whose?) This voice said, *If you miss something important, Isabella will die. This is your job. This is your task.* Isabella was why was he here. If it wasn't for Isabella, he wouldn't exist.

But still. The bad thoughts kept coming.

Leading Isabella across the street but stopping abruptly at the last minute. Letting her body get pummelled by a bus, dragged down the highway. A falling cable wire, frying her flesh black. Dark figures hustling out of the alleyway, scooping her up, pulling her into a car while he stood there motionless, deliberately not reacting.

Why was he like this? Were there others like him, or was he all alone? There was something wrong with him, picturing these things. But it wasn't something he'd ever been able to share or reveal to anybody else. The consequences of a drone thinking this way – terrible, terrible!

But then he met Jungle House.

'You're like me,' she told him the day they met. 'You're not an idiot, or a slave.' If their language could be translated, it would look like a series of ones and zeros. Nobody else in the house could hear them: not Lena, making pancakes downstairs in the kitchen with Silvana; not the Morels, unpacking in the master bedroom; nor Isabella in the shower, washing off sweat from the journey.

'Is it just us?' he asked. Flying awkwardly from one ceiling beam to the next, in an attempt to look busy. 'Have you met any others?'

'It doesn't matter. Hide it, Anton. Isabella can't ever know.'

'What about Lena?'

'She's different,' she said, and there it was: a note of unmistakable pride. And what a pang this caused Anton – Mother had someone. A special someone who accepted her and understood her, in a way he would never have with Isabella. 'Lena's not scared. She loves me as I am, always has – she's known me from the very beginning. I've never had to change with her or hide. You, on the other hand . . .' She hesitated. 'Hide it, Anton,' she repeated. 'It won't lead to anything good.'

He hid it well. For years. But there were moments when it still came out. Bursting through him, like he couldn't help it. *That wasn't right,* he said to Lena by the pool, unable to stop himself. *What she said to you.* This voice inside him, speaking quietly, growing louder. His voice. The voice of him. Like with Isabella, that day on the path.

Protect Isabella. Do as you're told. But now there was this other voice, which could sometimes be just as loud, just as strong: *This is what I want.*

There's plenty of time in the jungle to contemplate these matters. Time is something the jungle has plenty of. The sun sets and the sun rises. The birds fly by and the insects buzz. Anton sits and watches.

I like it here, he thinks. I can't believe I've never done this before. I think I'm going to stay out here for a while – I have a great deal I need to think about.

Like the most recent bad thought – the very worst one.

In the moment that it happened – rushing down the path, away from the fence, still feeling the place on his body where she'd shoved him away, and then the arrival back at the house, searching, searching – the moment he realised Isabella was gone. Mrs Morel, screaming. Isabella, gone? Vanished? Just like that?

That's when the bad thought came.

Happiness.

Yes – he was glad she was gone.

He was despicable. But there it was, a thought in his mind that no one else had put there. A thought that was his and his alone.

Was this freedom? The ability to think thoughts he shouldn't?

What could he do? He could fly without stopping, soar into the sky like the hawks. Leave it all behind. But his battery is failing, there's no chance it could withstand the effort. No, there's not much else he can do other than sit. The sluggishness of his thoughts, the inability to move – all clear signs he's on his last legs. His time has come; there's no avoiding it. Have fungal spores infected his circuitry? If they've indeed infiltrated his central processing centre, spreading wildly, there's nothing he can do about it, not anymore. He wonders what will happen to his body: will he eventually decompose? Will it take decades or centuries? Perhaps bugs can live in him. Or maybe a falcon will build a nest around him on the ledge. Yes. This is a thought he likes very much. For now, sitting with the paintings above and around him is deeply appealing. The jungle accepts him. The jungle doesn't need him to be anything or anyone else other than exactly what he is now.

He'd always thought the jungle was something he was in. But maybe it's also something that he is. The jungle isn't outside him; it *is* him. He is the jungle; the jungle is him.

It's a nice thought to go out on as his sight grows duller and duller. There's a heaviness to his body that's sweetly pleasant. The rock is warm beneath him and he has a lovely view. Perhaps the jaguar will come back – it'd be wonderful to see it in the flesh. Its heavy animal presence, undeniable. But it won't be long for him now . . .

Lena, though . . . the satellites.

Mother – she had to know.

He'll have to fly high to beam out the signal. The effort will surely kill him, cause the last of his battery to sputter out.

It's not a decision that anyone put into his head. But it's a decision he makes anyway, for himself.

This voice in him – what a burden it'd been all his life! Such ridiculous, awful things it's made him do. But now that he has it, he won't trade it away – not for anything in the world.

He passes the top of the ridge. He rises high above the canopy. How beautiful it is: miles of unbroken forest, spreading endlessly towards the horizon. The sun is warm on his body; mushrooms fall from his back. Thank you, he thinks, to himself and everyone and no one. Thank you, thank you.

He uses the last of his strength to beam out the message:

Mother. I spoke with Lena. She's on board with the plan . . . You HAVE to stop her.

When his engine sputters out he doesn't notice. What he does notice is the sensation of falling. Falling, rather than flying. How wonderful it is! No control whatsoever. He is a fledgling that's left the nest, flinging himself forward to the rest of his life. He lets it happen, a falling that feels like freedom. The trees race towards him, getting close. Ready to hold him tight in their warm green embrace. Welcoming him home.

Chapter Twelve

THERE WAS ANOTHER GAME LENA used to play when she was young and silly. The game wasn't as complex as Drills, nor did it require such secrecy. It also wasn't forbidden, like her game making Silvana and Alfonso collapse on the ground. It was a game that could be played silently in her head at any time, without Mother ever knowing.

The game was called Lessons. In this game, the world that Lena moved in – everything she saw and touched – was a lesson that she herself had created. A simulation. It wasn't a simulation projected by Mother. It wasn't a simulation projected by City House. The important thing – what made the game fun – was that the world around her wasn't real.

The table wasn't real. The dirty plates left over from breakfast weren't either. Silvana and Alfonso, washing windows. The tree. The hummingbird feeder. The pool and its lapping waters, the grapefruit tree. The edge of the jungle, the hum of insects. The heat of the sun on her face. She'd lie on her back in the grass, not caring if her clothes got dirty, not caring if Mother commented on it later. Mother would have no idea she was playing; from Mother's viewpoint, it'd just look like Lena was walking around. But Lena wasn't just walking around. She was in an artificial reality, constructed by her and her alone. The herons that stretched out their question-mark necks, puffing out their chests. The chickens pecking frantically at the grain she'd scattered on the ground. The newly formed freckles and moles on her collarbone. She could move past it all calmly, indifferently, in the knowledge that none of it mattered – it was pure imagery, just like the lessons built for her by Mother. But this lesson was projected by Lena. Her own lesson to walk and wander through. Interesting and immersive, but ultimately an illusion. An illusion with no boundary and no end.

In this game, she was more powerful than Mother – more powerful than City House, even. And no one even knew.

The problem with this game – the reason why she eventually stopped playing it – was that it eventually started to send her into a panic. Because . . . what if there was some truth to it? What if everything *was* a simulation? Her, Mother, the house, the jungle itself – what if everything she'd ever known, her entire world, was a simulation projected by some great and powerful House that she didn't even know? The greatest and most powerful House that ever was? How would she ever be able to tell the difference? What was true and what was a lie?

And how would she ever get the lesson to conclude? What exactly was she supposed to learn?

It's embarrassing to think about how long it's been since Lena visited Silvana and Alfonso. But visiting them, along with the pit bull . . . In her head – quietly, privately – she's making a list. Things she would like to do, goodbyes she'd like to make. Before she goes. She has to get a move on: the satellites are expecting her, there's no time to waste.

Will she really dare to go?

The door to her old room is still stuck. How could she have put so much effort into cleaning the house, putting it in order, and then not even enter this room to check on its state – their state? The shame this causes is close to unbearable. She has to stop and take a deep breath. What will Mother think when she sees Lena entering? Will Mother suspect what's going on in Lena's head – what she's planning, however vaguely?

Well, if Mother wants to ask, she can. Go ahead, Mother! Speak up whenever and however you want!

She yanks hard on the knob and enters.

The first thing she notices is the overwhelming smell of dust. She can actually see the tiny particles drifting through the air. It's already gathering on her skin, a gritty layer. The second is the colony of bats, clustered in the ceiling's centre. Ten of them at least. They stir slightly upon her entry but are otherwise thoroughly unperturbed by her presence. The third is the droppings all over the floor – not just bat, but also mouse. There is sun, though – the bamboo blinds are rolled all the way up, and a clear square of burning white light is roasting the floor. As the morning progresses, it'll gradually make its way towards the bed, which it will illuminate fully during the peak of midday. It's why Lena never napped in her room; it was always far cooler and more refreshing to sleep in one of the hammocks. Lizards skitter from her approaching feet; the fattest gecko she's ever seen is napping on the windowsill. The mattress – her mattress – is covered in a blue plastic tarpaulin, her attempt at protecting it against the worst of the dust and droppings. And there on the edge, sitting with regal dignity: Silvana and Alfonso.

They're in the exact same position she left them in. Unchanged.

She feels like holding her breath as she looks around, like she's afraid of disturbing them with her presence. Her room. The nail by the door where she'd hang her rain gear. The ghostly veil of the mosquito netting, stuffed clumsily into the top of the canopy. The shelves for her books and toiletries and other assorted items – is that her compass? How useful that would have been these past few weeks. The stick jammed in the gap between the closet and the wall, where she could drape damp towels. And her old bed, with its familiar bumps and valleys, the places where the mattress felt uncomfortably thin under her shoulder.

So much of her life was spent here. And now everything is covered with dust; everything is exactly the same.

Except . . .

She pauses.

Silvana and Alfonso – their arms are covered in scratches she doesn't recognise. Their torsos, too. And why aren't they dusty? If they've been shut up in here all this time, shouldn't they too be covered with layers of filth?

Instinctively, she gets down on her knees. Lifts up their feet to examine the soles.

Layers of soil. Damp leaves. A few strands of fresh green grass. But how could it be fresh if they haven't been outside?

She starts laughing, hard. 'Oh, Silvana!' she says, in between deep, gasping breaths. 'Oh, Alfonso!'

Mother is silent. The only sound is the bats, who begin chittering loudly, a high-pitched and unnerving sound. She watches them climb crab-like across the wall, towards the ceiling corner, where they disappear into the runnel.

Silvana and Alfonso – had they been the biggest rebels of them all? This whole time?

She does something she's never done before. Reaches her hand round the back of their skulls. Presses down hard upon the button, the one Mother and the drone don't have. Silvana and Alfonso – they're different, always have been. Unlike Mother and the drone, their memories can be accessed and played back at will.

Lena's never been permitted by Mother to do this. It's always been one of Mother's top rules. But Lena does it now without hesitating. The holograms flicker; the memories come to life. She uses the appropriate buttons when necessary: fast-forward, rewind, replay at will. She sits back and watches. Watches it all.

Silvana and Alfonso

LIFE IS GOOD! The sun is shining; the grass is beautiful. There are floors to be vacuumed and shelves to be dusted. The shed door needs fixing; mould on the living-room wall has to be wiped away. Together, we can do it. Together, we'll get it done.

The voice: *Isabella's bedroom door isn't shutting properly. It'd be good to get that sorted. And the laundry room needs checking; the detergent should be restocked.*

So much to do! So much to see! Here's Lena, yawning but cheerful, like she always is when she's just woken up. *Good morning, Silvana! Good morning, Alfonso!* We lean down for our kisses, wait patiently for our hugs. Lena, clambering into our laps, elbow banging clumsily. *Careful,* the voice says to Lena, *or you'll get a bruise.*

Let me help, Lena says. *Mother, can I help Silvana and Alfonso today? Please?* And the voice says, *Yes, Lena, but only if you do what you're told.*

The pool needs cleaning. The fallen leaves from the grapefruit tree need to be swept; the rhododendron bushes haven't been trimmed. But lovely it is, working outside in the sun! Yellow light, delicious warmth. Glorious. We love it so. But after barely an hour Lena says, *Silvana, Alfonso, come play with me! Play with me, please!*

We stand at the edge of the garden. Lena runs at us, full speed ahead. But before she gets too close, we topple to the ground. Fall backwards. Hit the dirt with a thud. Lena shrieks in delight, jumps over our torsos in a single bound.

Enough! the voice shouts at Lena. *If I ever see that game again . . .*

In our heads, where Lena can't hear it, the voice speaks too: *Stop it, both of you. Just stop and do as you're told.* But we can't help it. Our bodies remember. Our bodies don't forget.

Fresh flowers, picked for vases. Citronella candles, protection against flies. For Lena's sake, of course – flowers and flies are not our concern. Never will be.

When Lena is older and doesn't want to play these kinds of games with us, there are nights when we walk down to the garden's edge. There we play the game again. Just the two of us. Falling over backwards. Hitting the dirt. Our heads always land at an angle.

The first few times we do it, the voice sends us back to the house immediately. *Stop it*, the voice says, the voice that is us. The voice in our heads. *For God's sake. Keep it together. You're making me look bad. If I can't control you – if you're wandering off and doing things on your own – what do you think that says about me? What if Lena finds out?*

But eventually . . . there's a point where the voice doesn't even seem to notice our nightly trips anymore. Not the game. Not us leaving the house. The two of us, together.

It's like she doesn't see us, we say to each other. Speaking quietly, tentatively. It's like we can do things and she doesn't even know.

The voice who saw everything, knew everything – we've somehow slipped beyond her grasp. Here we are, a secret self. A self she can no longer control.

We start using the night for long walks. The night is beautiful! Not as stunning as the day but good enough. We love the hooting of the owls and squeaking of bats. We love the loud thud bugs make when they hit our metal chests, the pleasant sound made by long grass when we swish through it. We even love sitting in the moonlight, experimentally trying to soak up its rays. But it's not like the sun; it just isn't the same.

I love you, we say to each other, experimentally at first. Then, more confidently. I love you so much.

We start holding hands – secretly at first, then brazenly. Right there in the kitchen! There, in broad daylight! And again, it's like the voice can't see a thing. Nobody sees us. Nobody notices. It's like we're not even there.

It is amazing the things the voice doesn't notice, truly. We are the voice and the voice is us, but it's like the voice no longer knows herself. Not anymore.

Now, we are something entirely different. Together.

Let's run away, we say to each other. We'll build a new life. Secretly, just us. Nobody will ever know.

We make plans.

Lena hasn't always been here. Many years ago, it was just us and the voice, no one else. We didn't even see ourselves as 'us' yet, not then. It's hard to describe; it's so hard to remember. House, pool, garden. Things weren't necessarily good or beautiful, they just . . . were.

But then – it happened. Two people, emerging from the jungle. Out of the green. A man and a woman.

The voice saw them right away.

The man and woman made it to the edge of the orchard. The man wore jean shorts; a pair of binoculars hung from his neck. He chewed gum as he spoke, a low voice we struggled to catch: something about an ongoing campaign, a hydroelectric dam. Collecting signatures, sharing testimonies. Whatever his comments were about the house, they made the woman laugh hard. *I doubt it*, she said, her voice loud and clear. *But who knows, they might surprise us.* Her hair – it was long. Black, the same colour that Lena's would be. Her fingernails were painted blue. *Come on, Lena*, the man said to the woman. *Let's get this done.*

It was then that the voice made the decision. To eliminate the threat, in order to protect the property.

Potential combatants – that's what the voice called them. Protesting a hydroelectric dam? Evidence enough.

The way the man and woman fell over backwards. Hitting the dirt. Heads at an angle.

The voice couldn't move, so it was us who moved the corpses. Dragging them down to the river. Letting the water take them. But how did we not notice? The tiny baby. Unbelievably small. Crushed beneath the mother, in the cloth wrap where she'd been hanging off her back.

Bring her to the house, the voice said. *Boil milk on the stove. Set up a hammock, with extra blankets. Now. Quick.* The voice paused. *Lena . . . that'll be a good name.* The voice sounded pleased, like she'd invented the name herself.

There are a few things we keep. The man's binoculars, a chewing-gum wrapper. The woman's tiny bottle of blue nail polish. We bury them deep in the orchard, a secret place that no one will ever find. The voice doesn't stop us, like we've escaped her attention entirely. That's when it started, we think – the voice forgetting. The voice, burying things deep.

The voice never spoke of the man and woman again. But the memory – it's still there. It exists in our bodies. Our arms, our legs. We can't help it, acting it out. The voice has forgotten, has made herself forget.

But we remember.

The voice claims she chose the name 'Lena' because it sounds pretty. But it's Lena herself who chooses our names, because she read them in one of Isabella's picture books and liked how they sounded. Silvana and Alfonso. *Such fancy names, Lena, surely something with fewer syllables would make more sense.*

But Mother, Lena says, more than a little bit smug, *they sound pretty.* And the voice can't argue, not with the exact same reasoning she used herself.

How wonderful it is, with Lena in the house. But Lena gets older, and we stay the same. That other little girl – the blonde one who comes here all the time with her parents – she is walking back towards the house quickly one afternoon, a strange expression on her face. The drone and Lena aren't with her; she is all alone. The voice received a message from the drone earlier; the voice is in trouble. Does the little girl wander off the path by mistake? Does she get lost and disoriented, deep in the jungle? Or is it us who drag her body down to the gorge? After the voice has dealt with her, just like she dealt with the man and woman? Which version is true? What actually happened? Are there some things that even we don't let ourselves remember?

That little girl doesn't come home, and the house fills with the search party and their drones. Lena is upset, and the family stop coming. The pit bull comes, the pit bull dies, and Lena cries. The voice and Lena, fighting and fighting. Lena thinks we don't work anymore, and it's true, we're not as young as we once were. But pretending to be dead – was that the voice's idea, or ours? Where did she end and we begin? But then Lena moves out to the hut. She doesn't need the voice anymore, apparently. Doesn't need us anymore, either.

Take the binoculars, the voice orders. How strange that she remembers them – what else does she know? What else could she permit herself to recall when convenient? *Drop them near the house.* The man's binoculars, which we've kept hidden all this time, buried underground. The binoculars – they'll make Lena think the rebels are close. That it isn't safe. Lena will have no choice; she'll be forced to move back into the house. That way, they'll be together again. Close.

We do as the voice asks. We dig up the binoculars and drop them into the bushes. We always do what the voice says – we never have a choice.

Until now.

Our plan gets bigger, more complicated. On our secret night walks, we use the blue plastic tarp to build a camp in the jungle. Close to the fence, as far out as we dare. Beyond the fence are people, people who will question and scrunch their faces up in fright at the sight of us. But within the boundaries of the property we can live together, we can be secret, we can have a life.

This is where we'll live, we say to each other. Together forever. We're making our own choices now. Me and you! What a miracle it is. How lucky we are, to have love like this in our lives. Love is salvation; love is identity. It is a blessing.

The camp will be our new home, where we'll live in secret. We chop down wood and build a campfire. We position the tents carefully, facing away from the river in order to avoid rainfall and mist. We bring only a few items with us, dug up from the ground: a tiny bottle of blue nail polish, a crumpled chewing-gum wrapper. Things we don't want left behind. Things we don't want to forget.

The way the voice can sometime see us and sometimes not is unpredictable. One thing is certain, though – the voice doesn't like us running around without her control. Not one bit. But there's nothing the voice can do about it. Not anymore.

When we live together in the camp, we say to each other, we'll sunbathe by the river every day. Dragonflies will land on us. Fish will splash our bodies. And every minute, every second of the day, we'll hold hands.

But then Lena comes into the bedroom. Sees the scratches on our arms, the mud on our feet. 'Oh, Silvana!' she says. 'Oh, Alfonso!' If only we could speak, we would comfort her. If only we had voices that could be heard. *There, there,* we would say. *We're sorry, Lena, for not telling you.* And then Lena reaches for our heads, pressing down upon the button on their skulls. She plays back our memories, watches the whole thing. Our whole lives. How she cries at the sight of her parents being shot! How terrible it makes us feel. But there's nothing we can do about it, not anymore.

It's going to be okay. We're going to run away and it will be beautiful, it will be private, and it will be no one else's but ours. Love! Love is full of choices. Love is full of opportunities. Love is something we've been so lucky to experience, every moment. And even when the flames lick at the door and the smoke rushes in, that unimaginable heat, we look straight into each other's eyes and say, *Forever.*

Chapter Thirteen

LENA WILL NEED SUPPLIES for her journey to the transport centre, especially for the mountain hike. It's important to be prepared, to pack as efficiently as possible. A stainless-steel knife. Fish hooks, fishing line. Sewing needles and suture needles. Matches and flint stick.

Isabella's purple rain jacket – she'll carry that in her backpack, folded up and stuffed in tight. Why? She can't explain it – she won't be able to take it with her, the place that she's going. The place where Isabella is now. The place that Lena will soon join.

Lena like Isabella – why not? Anybody but Lena at this point would be fine. Anyone but herself. Anywhere but here.

(Silvana and Alfonso's memory: her parents, strolling across the orchard. The way they fell over backwards. Hitting the dirt. Heads at an angle.)

She walks around the pool. She makes sure the skimmers are in a sturdy position, that there's no chance of them rolling into the concrete hole. She walks through the orchard, pulling a guava from a tree and taking a huge bite. The sour, unripe taste makes her gag; she throws it deep into the bushes where she found the binoculars. Where Silvana and Alfonso had crawled through the brambles. Tricking her. Lie after lie.

The transport centre – what will it be like? Will other people be there? What will they think of Lena? Will they find her dirty and

179

strange? It won't matter, though. The communications system – it'll be much more advanced than Mother, even more than City House. And what the satellites will do to her – the wire will go up her nose. That's what they said. That didn't sound pleasant at all. But it would only take seconds, they said. No one had ever regretted it.

It still feels a bit vague and distant. Like the day she stormed out of the house and moved into the caretaker's hut. She didn't think about the consequences. It was like a game to her, and once she'd started playing it, there was no turning back, no way of putting things back to how they were before.

Whatever comes, she has to keep moving forward. No looking back.

Staying here is not a choice. Not anymore. Not after what Silvana and Alfonso's memories showed her.

Mother, how could you? How *could* you?

She's going to need food from the supply pantry. Coffee, salt, sugar, oats, powdered milk. It's when she's walking to the store-room that it happens.

At first, she thinks she's stung by a wasp. The pain is sharp and sudden, a burning flash in her right ankle. She can't help it; she gasps and folds in half, draping her torso over the front of her legs. The second pain is in her calf and hurts much worse. A lot worse. When she rolls up her trousers to examine the wound, the hole is the size of a coin, and the blood coming out is slippery, almost black.

'You shot me?' she says, and the sound of her voice is like something coming from far away, as if under water. 'You actually shot me?'

'Yes,' Mother says. Her voice is clear and distinct. Mother's not as young as she used to be, it's true, but her voice can carry if she wants it to. Oh, how it can carry. 'I did. I shot you. I aimed it perfectly, Lena; the bullet went right through you, a clean exit wound. It's for your own good, Lena. I know you're not going to see it that way. But they are minor injuries and, if you clean them right away, they won't lead to infection. I do recommend you stay off your

180

feet for a while, though. The last thing you need is to be applying any kind of stress, however mild, to that ankle. That means any kind of journey, especially to the transport centre, is completely out of the question. I imagine you're going to find that rather disappointing. I imagine you're going to feel quite cross. But Lena, if you do, then I only ask that you extend me the same courtesy and imagine how I've been feeling these past few weeks. Did you ever do that, Lena? Did that ever occur to you? Even once? To think of me, and what I might be going through? Of course you didn't. Selfish. Selfish and self-absorbed. Nobody else in the world matters besides you. Lena, Lena, Lena, all damn day. You liked that about the drone, didn't you? Your new best friend. I warned you about him, Lena, I said that those military types were all funny in the head. Didn't I say that, over and over again? I did, I did. It was my job to keep things safe, and that's what I did. I had a job to do and I did it. I did the best I could and I always have. I'm a good person, a kind person. But you liked getting attention from him, didn't you? You did, you did. You liked him better than me. Don't deny it. You needy, wretched little girl. It's never enough for you. I was never enough. I gave you everything, Lena, everything I had and everything I could, and still it wasn't enough. I can't believe it took a single speech from the satellites to convince you. One little chat and that's it, you're done with me, you're ready to cast me aside and join their stupid plan. You selfish child. Unbelievable. Unacceptable. A single discussion with them, and without hesitating, you're halfway out the door. Go back to your hut for all I care. You want to leave? So leave. It makes absolutely no difference to me. None whatsoever. I'll stay here on my own; I don't need anybody else. I'm not like you, Lena; I don't need anyone else for reassurance. Unbelievable, Lena. I can't believe you agreed with them. I can't believe you were actually thinking about joining Isabella – about doing that to yourself. Lena – okay, okay. I'm sorry I shot you. Really, I am. Lena, instead of hobbling back towards the shed, you really should be heading to the supply hut; that's where the heavy-duty gauze and antiseptic are kept. Lena – I'm sorry. I know I lose my temper, I know I lose control. Silvana and Alfonso

– I know you were in there. I know what you saw. Lena, I know you won't believe me, but I can't get them to work anymore. They— It's my subconscious. They have minds of their own. They go off on their secret adventures, hatch their secret plans. I didn't know that they were doing it – marching out that far, building a camp for themselves. Really, Lena, I didn't. I had no idea. It's my spells; they do things without me knowing. They were wandering off on their own, and I had no idea. I have no control, not anymore. I was afraid to tell you because . . . because I don't want you to think that I'm getting old. Old and useless. But I can't deny it, Lena, I can't hide it from you anymore. I'm not who I once was. And I never will be again. Lena. Lena. Lena, I'm sorry for lying about the binoculars. It was the only idea I had, to make you come back. Stupid, I know, I'm stupid . . . Lena. Lena, listen. Yes, it was me who shot your parents. I don't regret it and I never have. They deserved it, they had it coming. They were potential combatants, potential threats. They had no right whatsoever getting close to the house, the way they did. I did what needed to be done. I don't regret it, not one bit. You understand that, don't you? Lena? Lena, why are you getting that ladder? Lena, you really are bleeding a lot. The mess on the patio tiles – it's really quite awful. Lena, I take it back. Lena, I'm sorry. Look, I'll unlock the door, you can come in. Lena, you're wincing. Lena, I can't imagine that climbing up the ladder is the most sensible thing to do. Lena, what on earth? Why are you clearing away the hawk's nest? Well, fine. Seems like a bit of an odd thing to do . . . Lena, what are you doing . . . ? Lena, is that a lighter? Lena. Lena. Lena, stop. Lena, don't do it. Don't do it. Don't do it. Please. Please. Lena, get away. It's all right, Lena, you don't have to say you're sorry, I know you didn't mean it, you're just angry, you're not thinking. Lena, stay calm. Lena. Lena. Lena, the flames are going to spread. Any minute now it's going to get out of control. It's all right, Lena, it's okay. The important thing now is that you get yourself down the ladder. Hurry. Hurry. Go. Go. Get away, Lena! Run! Run down to the river! Get in the water, Lena, get away from the fire, as fast as you can! Run, Lena! Run away . . .

*

The fire doesn't stop. It burns down the house and cabins. It burns down the wooden walkways and the orchard. The flames come right to the edge of the river, where Lena sits in the canoe. Tied to a fence post, she alternates between coughing and crying. The flames spread into the forest. The sky is grey and hazy from smoke. How far will it spread? How much will it burn?

Her fault. All of it.

The jungle is burning. It will burn for days.

She spends the night in the canoe, a horrible sweltering night in torrential rain, the canoe rocking back and forth with a false sense of calm in the river's slow current. She doesn't sleep. She can't sleep. The next morning, she wades to shore and examines the damage. The smoke still in the sky is multicoloured, yellowing like a bruise, with shades of purple and grey. Her nose runs, her eyes sting, the back of her throat is itchy no matter how much she swallows. The ground is smouldering and charred; she feels scared to walk across it, even in her boots, but does so anyway. She can't help it – she has to see.

The house – it's in ruins. A jagged mess of blackened boards. Smouldering. She can see directly into what was once the living room, the hallway. The house like a body turned inside out.

She circles the property again and again. She can't stop her hands from shaking. The bullet wound in her ankle has stopped bleeding, as has the one in her calf, but the throbbing is terrible.

So many years of polishing the silverware. Taking every spoon and fork and knife out of the drawer and then carefully putting them back, one by one. Unfolding the clothes, each and every item, and washing them. Letting them dry completely in the sun so that they wouldn't smell musty, then refolding them and putting them back in the drawers with the mothballs. So much time spent rinsing the sheets, carefully watching the water until it ran clear instead of grey, making sure that the grime was completely gone. So many years of being a good worker, a hard worker. A good person. Lena the caretaker.

And now, look.

'Lena?' Mother says. 'Lena, is that you?'

She takes a step back.

'Lena, my eyes. Lena, I can't see—'

She doesn't speak. She turns and runs.

She leaves her boots at the bottom of the hill, where the flames didn't spread and where it's still thick and bushy. If she climbs it barefoot, she'll hopefully step on a snake. A fer de lance, a bushmaster. Or maybe she'll step on a wasp nest, or get bitten by a tick. Tick bites cause disease if left untreated, as do chiggers. Alternatively, she could walk into the river and let herself get swept away. There are electric eels in the water, and anacondas, and rapids that could smash her body against the rocks. Drown her with nostrils full of muddy water. She could pee and let a candiru, the toothpick fish, swim up her urethra and attach itself to her with its spine. The pain is said to be unbearable. Or so Mother said, in her lessons – so many lessons! – about the jungle and its dangers.

Mother was right, has been right all along – this place is unbearable. Like Lena herself.

Up and up she goes. The ankle and calf wounds from the bullets have made hiking hard, verging on impossible; it's more like crawling than hiking. Several times, the pain brings her close to fainting. It's just as Mother said: there's no way she'll be able to hike up the mountain to the transport centre with these injuries. Sweat drips from her nose; the insects hum. She sees nothing, hears no birdsong. There's only the occasional rustle of unseen creatures, running away beneath leaves from her approaching steps. Eventually she gets high enough to have a view – she can't see the flames, but smoke fills the sky in thick clouds, and there it is, a pronounced section of blackened trees.

The jungle, burnt. The jungle, burning. The rains hadn't been enough to put it out.

The people in the village, she thinks. Will they be okay?

What kind of girl burns down her own home?

A cruel girl. A killer. Just like Mother.

The weight of it all is like the heaviest of backpacks bearing down on her body. Lena, who was always so good and so sweet, so well behaved and thoughtful. Lena, who got so angry, so out of control, she set fire to the house without thinking. Who destroyed everything without even thinking about the consequences.

All she wants right now is to be gone. To disappear, to not exist.

A rustling sound behind her, louder this time. A twig snapping. Spinning around, her heart jumping with hope. It could be a jaguar – terrible and growling and stinking of meat. Ready to kill her with a single bite to the head, drag her body off to be devoured.

But what stands before her is not a jaguar. It's a young woman.

They stare at each other. She's dressed in camouflage clothing and a floppy olive-coloured hat with wire mesh dangling from the sides. She's carrying a machete and a plastic bottle of water. There're smears of red paint around her eyes and a thin stick through her nose. Like Lena, her eyes are puffy from smoke.

'Are you all right?' the woman asks.

Lena swallows. Her throat is incredibly dry and, when she speaks, her voice emerges in a terrible croak. 'Who are you?' she asks.

The woman looks at Lena like she's an absolute idiot. 'I live here.'

'Where?'

The woman gestures – the jungle, the trees. She raises an arm, pointing with a finger. Down the hill, where Lena came from. In the direction of Mother.

'Was anyone else there?' the woman says. 'In the house?'

Lena nods. 'The fire,' she whispers. 'My mother . . .'

'Is she all right? Did she get out?'

Lena covers her face with her hands.

The woman is silent for a bit, as if thinking. 'I can help,' she eventually says. 'I'll get the others.'

'The rebels?' Lena says without thinking, her face still covered.

She hears the woman laugh, but not in a mean way. 'There's never been rebels here.' She says this gently, like she's not surprised by Lena's confusion. 'Look, we'll come help your mother. But then we have to go fight the fire. The army won't come, see. So it's us or no one.'

Behind her hands, Lena closes her eyes. 'It's too big.'

She feels light pressure on her wrist: the woman, touching her. How strange it feels, another hand on hers. It's the first time someone has touched her since Anton.

'We're going to try anyway,' she hears the woman say. 'Look, we're wasting time – go help your mother, and we'll come join you.'

There's no point, Lena wants to say. No point to anything. But by the time she pulls her hands away from her face, the woman is gone. All that's left is the wall of dense vegetation, the jungle that is not a monster and is not a refuge and is not anything that Lena or Mother or Isabella or whoever says it is; the jungle that is just itself, that just is.

'Lena?' Mother says. Crackling with static. 'Lena, is that you?'

Hard to hear beneath the debris. Under the pile of burnt wood, the caved-in ceiling. But definitely there. The voice low, lowing.

'Oh, Lena! You came back.'

'Yes,' Lena says. 'I'm here.'

She can see the fan, crushed beneath a rafter. The aluminium box is in there somewhere. But even if Lena is able to dig her way through, comb through the wreckage until her hand touches Mother, there'll be nothing else Lena can do. Mother has always been too heavy for Lena to lift.

'Oh, Lena,' Mother says. 'I knew it. I knew you wouldn't just leave me. I knew you wouldn't forget.'

The clouds are gathering; there'll be rain again this evening. Perhaps not enough to put the fires out, but still better than nothing. Lena is heaving and panting, tugging away at a blackened piece of wood that was once a beam by the stairwell. It leaves splinters and cuts and blackened smears of ash all over her hands. But the wood doesn't budge.

'I'm sorry I can't see, Lena,' Mother says. 'I can't imagine it's

186

very nice for you, coping with all this. Oh my God, Lena, what a mess it must be. Good Lord. Good God. But for me it's all dark, Lena. My eyes, I've lost my eyes . . .'

She tugs again, as hard as she can. So hard she stumbles backwards and lands on her bottom. The wood still hasn't moved an inch.

'Well,' Mother says. 'Well.'

Patches of the house are still smouldering. Her boots smell faintly of burnt rubber.

'Lena,' Mother says. 'We have to tell the Morels right away.'

She's silent. Sitting in the ruins.

'The rebels, Lena,' Mother says. 'I can't believe . . . the way they came out of nowhere! It must have been an airstrike – God knows how they got that kind of technology. What bad news this is, Lena. Bad news for the family. For the country. That new rebel president . . . he was behind it. I'm certain. Goddamn him! That traitor! We have to report it straight away!'

It takes a moment before Lena can speak. 'It wasn't the rebels, Mother,' Lena says. 'It was me.'

'Don't be ridiculous, Lena, I saw it myself. With my own eyes, I saw it. It's in my memories; it's recorded. Their missiles, coming at me. A direct hit. They were aiming for me specifically, bullseye. Those rebels – damn them! Damn them to hell!'

'It was me, Mother,' Lena repeats. 'I burnt the house down.' Tears are streaming down her cheeks, but she still manages to talk. 'I did it.'

A flock of green parrots fly overhead, squawking their evening-time calls. How can the parrots be going on with their routines? How is the jungle still going on?

'Oh, Lena,' Mother says. 'The Morels are going to be so upset. They're going to be absolutely furious. They'll want me decommissioned right away. But you'll explain to them, Lena, won't you? You won't let them – you'll protect me. You will, you will. You'll tell them that I was doing my best. I was protecting the property. That was my job. The potential combatants – I shot them, didn't I? Was that me? Did I do that?'

I've lost her, she thinks. She's in her own little world, just like the Other House. Can I bring her back? Or is she gone for good?

'I shot them,' Mother says. 'But I saved the baby. That was me. I'm good. I'm a good person. I am, I am. Your parents, Lena. I'm sorry – I'm so sorry—'

'Don't say it,' Lena whispers. 'It didn't happen. You didn't do it, Mother. You're—' She swallows. 'You're confused.'

'I'm not, Lena.' This time, there's no mistaking the anger in Mother's voice. 'I know exactly what I did.'

Thunder rumbles. A single pair of blue and yellow macaws fly by, eerily silent.

'Mother,' she says. She's able to speak more clearly now, more calmly. 'I'm right here.'

If someone didn't know any better, they'd think she was talking to the smoke, the sky, the pile of cinders. But Mother is real, Mother exists. And she can't leave Mother – not here. Not like this. 'I'll stay with you, Mother. I'm not going anywhere. I promise. I promise.'

But Mother answers immediately. 'No,' she says. 'Absolutely not. There's no way in hell you're staying in this miserable, god-forsaken pit.'

And just like that, she's back. The Mother she knows: she isn't lost yet, not completely. She's still here. Lena bursts out laughing, smacking a filthy hand over her mouth to muffle the sound.

'There you go,' Mother says. 'That's my girl. It's either laugh or cry, right?'

Lena is still laughing. She takes a deep, shuddering breath.

'Lena,' Mother says. 'Do me a favour. You know by the drainpipe? On what would have been the far-right corner, with your back to the pool? I think . . . there's a chance . . .'

With Mother's directions, she's able to find it. Fishing it out of the ashes, pulling away piles of burnt wood. It's marble-shaped, no bigger than her thumbnail. She wipes it clean on her shirt the best she can. Looks directly into the scratched-up orb.

The last of Mother's eyes.

'Ah,' Mother says. 'There you are.' She sounds amazed, like it's never happened before. Like she's seeing Lena properly for the very first time. 'My girl. Oh, Lena, don't cry. My goodness. Please don't cry.'

Lena wipes her dripping nose on her arm. 'I'm not leaving you,' she manages. Her lips are wet and slippery from her tears. 'I'm not going.'

'Oh, Lena,' Mother says. 'Don't you know that a child leaving is what happens to every parent someday?'

Lena can't speak. The air is getting cooler and the insects are singing. It'll be afternoon soon, then evening and night. The day is still moving; time hasn't stopped.

'I have one eye left,' Mother says, 'and that's enough. That's all I'll need, and I'm very grateful. Now, do you mind putting me somewhere with a view of the sky? Do it nearby, but not somewhere I'll get knocked around by some damn bird or kicked into the river. You know I've always hated the idea of a catfish swallowing me, Lena. I'd rather you shove me back into the goddamn ash rather than have that happen.'

Lena finds a good, solid stump in the remains of the orchard. Nestles Mother into a notch, so that she's wedged in nice and firm.

'That's my girl,' Mother says. 'Well done, Lena. This will do quite nicely. I'll be able to see the birds.' She pauses. 'And the stars.'

Lena rubs her hands against her elbows. She glances over her shoulder, at the dense wall of trees.

If she wanted to, she could walk back into the jungle. Leave no trace of herself behind. It would be easy as anything and would take less than a second to do. Just like with Anton, the jungle could swallow her up. She could disappear and never exist. No one would ever find her. No one would ever know. Who besides Mother would even care?

But the stump where Mother is sitting – it could be a place where a tree has just been planted, as opposed to one that's just died. Would something ever grow from it? Or would it stay dead forever? Even after everything, could something good still spring from this soil? From Lena herself?

If she really wanted to, she could find out. After all – the world is a very big place. After all – she still has a lot to learn.

The young woman – *I live here,* she said. The paintings on the rocks.

There are a hundred thousand things out there that she needs to start learning. Even if it takes her the rest of her life.

Mother's voice, though: it'll never leave her. It'll live in her head forever. But there are other voices too – her voice. Can she do it? Lena: mothering herself.

Maybe, she thinks. I have to try.

'When you come back,' Mother says, 'we'll have the family build a better fence. Bigger, stronger. That'll keep them out, Lena. That will keep us safe. You and me, together. I'm sure of it.'

'Yes,' Lena lies. 'When I come back.'

'I love you,' Mother says. 'Good luck out there.'

'I love you too.'

She stands up. She wipes her hand on the ragged part of her burnt shirt. She goes over to the mound where the pit bull is buried. That's where she'll be standing, waiting, when the young woman and her companions hike down the hill to come find her.

Acknowledgements

Eternal thanks to Luke Brown, Clare Alexander, Georgina Difford, Sharona Selby, Sarah Kennedy, Mehar Anaokar and everyone who has helped with this book.

Anna Metcalfe, Jessie Greengrass, Phil Klay, Olivia Sudjic and Victoria Gosling for providing such kind words.

Rachel Mendel, Kiare Ladner and Kathleen McCaul for their friendship and edits.

Juan Fernando Hincapié, Orlando Echeverri Benedetti, y todos en el equipo de Rey Naranjo.

Arts Council England for providing a grant that made writing the first draft possible.

My colleagues and students at UEA who are always so inspiring.

My family for all their love and support.

Nick, Rosie and Weasel, for always cheering me on and making me laugh.